THE

OCEAN

CONTAINER

THE

OCEAN

CONTAINER

Patrik Sampler

ninebark

ISBN-13: 978-0-9791320-4-9
ISBN-10: 0-9791320-4-5

Cover Design: Lou Robinson
Book Design: Hailey Rabdau

ninebark

Rome, GA & Salt Lake City, UT
ninebarkpress.org

Ninebark Press is sponsored by the Rome Area Council for the
Arts. Tax-deductible contributions designated for Ninebark Press
may be addressed to Ninebark Press/RACA, 3 Central Plaza, Suite
359, Rome, GA 30161.

CONTENTS

PART ZERO

Attention equals life or is its only evidence.

FRANK O'HARA

What can I see?

Thin mist blowing through the branches of wind-carved Sitka spruce, cracked, grey bark and thin lower branches hung with a wispy lichen known as *speckled horsehair*. (I'm using *your* names for these things because I don't have my own, and I want you to understand.)

At the base of these trees are some salal bushes, ripe with purple berries, beyond my reach. Below them are deer ferns, and a variety of other low-growing plants, which from my vantage point seem almost *tropical*. Like an Henri Rousseau jungle. It's an observation you, too, might make—if you were this low to the ground. You might see it this way despite knowing the latitude is too far north for a jungle. 53° north.

The mist alternately accumulates and thins. When it's thin and the light is right, dew sparkles, berries glow, and the various greens are distinct from one another. Sometimes, when there are gaps in the mist, one can see a faint blue sky. To you, it would be the same colour blue as a 1956 Buick Special. A colour known as *chalfonte blue*.

Within the groundcover is a tiny rose-like plant—a dewberry with a single raspberry-like drupelet atop its central stem. I can see it from the interior corner of my left eye. It is a miniscule prize, and for this reason rarely harvested. To me it is worth everything, and I attempt to reorient my body in order to grasp it between my thin, prehensile lips. With great effort I succeed, and am able to vacuum its meager juices through my keratin filter teeth.

It is the last thing I eat.

I was stranded

Prior to the dewberry, I had eaten nothing for many days. I have eaten nothing since. And yet when I came here the food was plentiful. There were ripe salal berries at water level, and I plucked them. I stirred up the bed of what was—temporarily—a saltwater lake. I opened my jaw, filled my mouth, strained out the water, and ingested a bounty of sand fleas, small fish, and even the odd *sandpiper*—a kind of bird. Some of them had washed inland during the upheaval. I needed to compress them in my mouth so they could slide freely down my gullet. I heard their little bones snap like dry twigs.

There had been great turbulence, and I know now that my inland access was granted by a tsunami. It was one of the tsunamis referenced in oral histories of the first people to inhabit the area. It is estimated to have taken place sometime in the fifteenth century, but I can tell you with certainty it washed ashore at 2:23 pm on August 24, 1426.

I swam into what I thought was an inlet—in fact an inshore basin, its access to the ocean only temporary. I swam around for a few days, but couldn't find my way out. It hardly mattered at first, what with the plentiful nourishment. But then the water levels subsided and I couldn't swim at all. And now there is no water—just mist and damp. I know I won't survive.

The spot at which I rest—from which I am unable to move—is the same spot at which I extruded the last major meal to occupy my bowels. Flies feed on my excrement, and they will soon feed on my flesh. I have reported the visual splendor of this place, but now my eyes have clouded over. I see almost nothing.

My internal organs are being compressed under their full terrestrial weight. My heart pumps with great effort, and I have lost most of my fat reserves. My skin is cracked and painful. And I am very cold—as cold as you would be if you were naked, floating in the North Pacific. The air temperature here should be no colder than the nearby water, yet I feel no warmth. Nor do I have, any longer, the strength to shiver.

It is sad to know my body—*this life*—will soon expire. It is also frustrating: I can hear the waves crashing against the shore. The ocean is not far away. And yet I have been unable to find my way back.

driftwood

One day a person will walk through this forest and see what looks like a small piece of driftwood. They will wonder how a piece of driftwood found its way so far inland. They won't recognize it for the jawbone of a whale. Of course they won't. No one would expect the jawbone of a whale to be *so small*.

If there were a name for my species, it might be *super-pygmy blue whale*. That is because we are exactly like blue whales—like scale models of blue whales. The largest of our species is perhaps only two metres in length. We evolved to this size the last time atmospheric CO_2 levels were above 400 parts per million, roughly one million years ago. Our food supply dwindled and we couldn't sustain our weight. We lost body mass just as salamanders and other species are doing in your time. Or so the theory goes.

I know you might not believe such a species as the *super-pygmy blue whale* ever existed. Perhaps it is because you possess discrete knowledge of the evolution of whales generally. You may doubt that a species such as ours—some 46 million years removed from our ancient ancestor *maiacetus*'s first experiments with life in the water—could have evolved and disappeared so quickly. But whatever your level of knowledge, I ask you not to doubt. Just let it be. Trust me when I tell you: *we existed*. Trust me also when I tell you: *I have since been reincarnated many times, and am still on this planet.*

PART ONE

Solitude is liberty indeed, bounded only by the obsessive appetite and the animal lust to roam.

CHRISTOPHER BURNEY, *SOLITARY CONFINEMENT*

I'm still thinking of the things I left on the coffee table: a small plate with a slice of buttered soda bread, a half-consumed (and very strong) Americano, and my smart phone. It was the Saturday following the election, late morning. I was in New Westminster, at my family's half of a very old house (in a style known as *early vernacular*), which had been converted to a duplex.

"You've got to leave now."

That's Janet, another NGO careerist, and someone helpful in my rise as a hope-peddler and junketeer. She'd arrived unexpectedly, and was telling me to leave my house—at least for now. Or perhaps not just for now.

"You heard what Fucker said about 'economic impediments,' 'terrorism,' and all that. They're not messing around this time," she said.

It wasn't really news, but it raised a number of questions similar to those one might ask during an earthquake, at the onset of shaking. Will it get worse? If it continues, how long should I wait before taking cover under a table? Do I have enough time to finish my coffee before I have to *do something*?

"I'm not messing around this time, either. You have to trust me."

"Do I have enough time to brush my teeth?"

"Probably. But not much more."

"Where are we going?"

She asked for my smart phone and I gave it to her. She erased all my contacts, messages, passwords, and photos—she told me that's what she was doing. Then she put the phone down on the table.

"It's probably not serious enough they'll send someone to tail us— not physically. For now they'll think you're here with your phone. Do you have any subdermals?"

"What do you mean?"

"Like they got for the FaceWatch Visa accounts. I know you don't, but I have to ask."

Yoshiko and Stevie were away, visiting family in Japan. And we had, by coincidence, an earthquake kit—in a gym bag near the back door. Which made it easy to leave. Quickly, that is. Not that I felt the urgency—not in a visceral way. Simply, it seemed prudent to trust someone who, as far as I knew, had always shown good judgment.

election results

In the twenty-first century there is still a ritual known as a *general election*, not to be confused with *democracy*—whatever that means. Just days before my evacuation we were in the midst of such an election. I went down to the campaign office expecting a party, but just minutes after the polls closed, the result was clear. The office—barren space rented at a strip mall—became an elevator in sudden descent.

Someone asked: "Did you feel that?"

Another voice said: "It's rigged."

I thought: perhaps.

We were in an elevator with glossy, dark wood panels affixed to stainless steel interior walls. Not real wood, but wood-laminate: the kind that denoted cheapness in my youth, but was chic—made new again—in the second decade of the twenty-first century. Was it chic this time, or merely fake? Did anyone care?

Prior to the election, I'd thought something had to change, if only for the sake of change. I never trusted there would be an informed result, just that change would happen—sometime. My theory was this: after so many years, regardless of whether a government is good or bad (in this case it was bad), inevitably people get bored of it and vote for a different one. There was precedent for this theory, so I expected to celebrate, or at least to feel relieved.

But rather than getting what I expected, I made a discovery: that people just wanted the same. That at this point in history, anyway, they want things *just the way they are*—which is something new. It's

Eno and Schmidt, Oblique Strategy 81 (sinister): "Repetition is a form of change." A *eureka moment*, as they say.

So twenty minutes after the party was supposed to start I was driving home. And I was worried, although I had been worried before. To be sure—as far as I knew at the time—I could still make my mortgage payments, and I owned my car. I thought: they wouldn't outlaw me and take away all my precious stuff, would they? Until then they hadn't, and why should they, if my consumer rights are worth more than my status as a dissident? Isn't that what the Prime Minister said? "We're all Executives now." Then he named this country Economy—which means *money*.

My car, incidentally, was bought used and cheap—an electric hybrid, suitable for the public image of an environmentalist. A car to take Yoshiko and Stevie on island road trips in the summer. Hard, Toyota-grade, recycled plastic dashboard, which was supposed to be a selling point. Instead it gave the impression of something needing to be thrown away—*as quickly as possible*.

But enough about me and my car: while I was driving away from the campaign office, someone else entirely—someone unconnected to the party I had just left—was going home in a chauffeur-driven Audi S7, extended wheelbase. Extra legroom and *real wood*. A built-in martini kit, perhaps? He'd considered a Rolls-Royce Phantom, but didn't want to go too flashy.

I was a baby

It may be important to acknowledge here that, many years before this, I was a newborn baby. It was my son, Stevie, who helped me understand that I too had been a baby, and then a small child. I'm thinking of little Stevie as a newborn, his unfocused gaze like that of a *Butoh* dancer in a slow, meditative sequence. What did those eyes see but perhaps a Turneresque wash of colour? And later his little hands. I'm thinking of Stevie touching my face. At first with only tactile interest. Next with moderation, as he learned *not to touch others in a way that would be unpleasant for them*. Finally it was with pride, as he learned the word for each part. I needed time to unmerge myself from the world, too, to see that others were distinct from me. Like Stevie, I also had little hands. And as I became mobile, I needed someone to make sure I didn't cause harm—to myself in particular.

Now I am a middle-aged man, unsure I can return to that oceanic state. Stevie is very far away—across an ocean. And in my current circumstances, it may be dangerous to step out to find him.

the shipping container

The identification code for my shipping container is TSCU8363946. I believe a part of this code refers to a company that owned or currently owns it: perhaps I can't truly say the container is *mine*. Nor do I know how it arrived at its current location. It may have arrived by truck, or it may have arrived by train. It's located near a railway sorting yard, so probably the latter.

The shipping container in which I live is, properly, an *intermodal freight container*. In this case, it is the shortest standard length: 20 feet. The standards for such things were developed in the United States, and thus were determined using imperial measurements. (Elsewhere I shall use metric.) Anyway, the smaller size is an advantage, as it's easier to heat. The container is not insulated, and I have taken residency in the winter.

I have access, by way of an extension cord, to an undependable source of electricity. To this I have connected an oil-filled radiator. For backup (when the electricity fails) I have a propane convection heater, which—when I use it—needs to be placed by the door, kept open a crack to vent the fumes. I prefer not to use it.

My shipping container has very few modifications, and no windows. When the doors are shut, the only source of light is an IKEA work lamp (a model I believe is called Kroby). When this lamp fails, I have a number of mechanically charged flashlights, which I hang from adhesive hooks on the corrugated steel walls.

The floor is plywood, and on it I have placed an inflatable mattress and sleeping bag, two yellow plastic milk crates, a backpack, and a number of plastic bags in which I keep personal items, including the notebook in which these thoughts are recorded.

the safety compound

The owner of shipping container TSCU8363946—if it still has an owner—will know its current location: a *safety compound* near an estuary on a fjord north of Vancouver. It's an ominously claustrophobic location: a low, flat area walled by mountains so close they appear at all times as if viewed through binoculars. With just a narrow window to an inland sea, the place is generally in shadow—for most of the day, for most of the year.

It rains frequently, and if I ever leave this place I will take away an image of white plastic furniture, dirt collecting in the seats of chairs, brown plastic ashtrays on tabletops, rain drops splashing in the ashtrays, cigarette butts floating. Red, green, and blue shipping containers, tents on wood pallets, portable canopies covering some of these. Mud, and bark mulch.

For some readers, it will be important to know—for me to convey with *some realism*—the route taken from my house in New Westminster, where Janet found me, to the safety compound. First of all, despite her doubts we would *physically* be followed, she took precautions. In short, we went to a Greek restaurant in an old cinder-block strip mall off Davie Street in Vancouver (but not the unjustifiably popular one you might be thinking of). There we met Dave, another close friend. After a disarmingly jovial lunch, Dave took my jacket and I took his coat. (We share a similar physique.) Next, Dave left out the front door with Janet, and I left out the back, where I was met by a vehicle—a grey, first-generation Ford Transit Connect—driven by a man I didn't know. I introduced myself.

"Hello."

"Hello."

"I'm—"

"Not interested," he said. "If I'm questioned, don't want anything to report. Don't give your deets to anyone."

the safety compound 2

More important than how I got to the safety compound (finally, under a rip in a chain-link fence, key in hand and verbal directions memorized) is the way such places work. Generally speaking, *safety* is a euphemism here—referring only ostensibly to the safety of those inside. These places are essentially walled tent and container villages, with ID required to enter—and to leave.

How did they come to be?

To begin with, there were large numbers of homeless people. Concurrently there were old prohibitions on vagrancy, and newer prohibitions on feeding vagrants. There were few places available to house the homeless indoors, but lots of charity organizations providing meals, medical advice, and menial jobs—collecting discarded bottles and cigarette butts, for example.

Ultimately, vacant property was sanctioned as space in which the homeless could pitch their tents. Fences were put up to prevent overspill. Then gates were installed, and a pass entry system developed to keep the homeless safe from gang violence and such like. Charity providers were favourable to the convenience of operating in centralized locations. Gradually these charities became silent on the prospect of ending homelessness, and emphasized *community economic development* within the compounds themselves. To keep the *criminal element* away, FaceWatch verification became an entry and exit requirement. Privacy concerns were raised but largely ignored—if people knew of them at all.

The safety compound in which I am located has all variety of charity. Freight companies provide old or currently vacant containers. A food bank distributes packaged meals. Students from a hairdressing school visit to practise their skills. Law students help those who are interested sign up for FaceWatch accounts. Something called the Homeless Empowerment Network pays for electricity. Artists entertain, and attempt to engage us with *theatre of the oppressed* and other such strategies—although no one seems to give a shit.

The charities see themselves setting up something like Christiania, the Danish commune. But they tend to overlook the gated element: the safety compound has more in common with Gaza. And most of the occupants—especially the newly displaced—are in denial. They say, "Now I know how it feels to be homeless." They do not say, "Now I am homeless."

pilings

I think I am homeless now—or at least I am now on the outside of five very good years. During that time I moved in with Yoshiko, I secured a place at the top of EcoRights, and Stevie was born. It's easy to say things were better before I was forced into hiding, but Yoshiko and Stevie really did make life lighter for me—lighter and *limitless-feeling*, even. Being without a home is not like that at all.

I remember as a child—and even later—playing a private game in which I trailed an imaginary line behind me, altering my path so it wouldn't catch or be tangled with anything. I haven't given much thought to why that game originated, but during the past five years I imagined a different kind of line, one that stretched out in front of me, like something to reel in. More accurately it was a line along which I pulled myself forward, along a path of happy circumstances, expecting them never to end. After the election, after Yoshiko and Stevie leaving for Japan, after my internment, I would say the line has brought me to a shore. I wade in, only to find the line tangled up in pilings. I go no further.

others in the compound

Despite my isolation I observe, fleetingly, others who inhabit the compound—especially if they are active near my container. Such is the case one evening when I am disturbed by the following loud interaction:

"C'mon buddy."

"What the fuck is it?"

"Here, little buddy!"

"Wouldn't say 'little'. It's some kinda elephant pig or somethin'."

(Whooping and whistling.)

Peering out my door, I see three young men dressed in track top, jeans, and sneaker combinations, and a young woman in thin tights, powwow boots, and a blouson with an exaggeratedly large fur-trimmed hood. Two of the young men are holding cigarettes, the ends of which glow in the fading light. They have cornered an animal, which stands frozen against a fence at the end of my container alley. In silhouette the animal indeed looks like a pig—although its snout is much longer.

One of the men picks up something to throw at the creature, which lets out a high-pitched squeal—surprisingly high for an animal of its size, and too high for a pig. The animal bolts suddenly down the length of the fence.

"Gross!" yells the young woman.

"What is that? Did it fuckin' piss on you?"

One of the young men laughs.

"Don't fuckin' laugh at 'er, fuck," says another. "If you laugh at 'er again I'll fuckin'...." His speech is slurred, and he is perhaps *too far gone* to complete the thought.

The four disperse.

toilets

You may have wondered about the compound's basic infrastructure. Do we have potable water? Are there showers? Are there laundry facilities? How do we leave our shit here in the compound, and where does it go? If you guess there is no sewage system, you are correct. It would also be correct to assume that, despite our marginalization, it's in no one's interest, really, to leave us without facilities—so the Homeless Empowerment Network has rented some portable toilets.

The toilet stalls are made from slightly translucent, baby blue fibreglass. On a sunny day they are bright enough inside that a flashlight isn't required. If one has time, one can appreciate the uniqueness of the patterned fibreglass. It is the chopped variety, its overlapping fragments as pleasing to my eyes as stained glass, a kind of geometric abstraction, reminding me of Marc Chagall's *Peace Window*—the one he designed for the United Nations. I saw it once when I was in New York, on a junket trip to some kind of environmental conference.

Anyway, because it is winter these outhouses are very cold—not that I mind. Each is at a comfortable distance from the next, and I would rather evacuate my bowels here than in the warm and intimate toilet stall of an under-ventilated, underground, ceramic-tiled washroom with brown-stained grout. In such washrooms one can hear, in neighbouring stalls, the sound of strangers' turds caressed out of sphincters, and one can smell warm odours.

The only complaint I have about the compound outhouses is that sometimes I run out of toilet paper—if, say, I have had a good food supply, or am particularly shitty that day. Everyone must bring their own toilet paper. For those who have none, there is a supply of old newspapers.

On one visit, I find a section of *The Globe and Mail*. A marketing firm has surveyed print media across thirty-six "developed countries," comparing advertising revenue to reported disasters by nationality. Americans, I learn, "represent consistently high value per capita," as do British and Australians.

my son and the future

Alone in my container, I'm thinking of the joy our little Stevie takes in life. His joy in being chased around the house, and his unrestrained laughter when I bounce him on the bed and pretend to gobble him up, as if I am a monster. In the city, he points out every bus he sees—"Bish! Bish!"—and is proud to climb steps on his own. As often as we find time, he is in the forest, where he is curious to feel the textures of bark on various trees— western red cedar, Douglas fir, arbutus. Just days after his birth, I took Stevie outside for a walk in our neighbourhood. He was born in the fall, when the autumn leaves were at their most vibrant. I saved one of those leaves, pressed it, and put it in a box, which I stored in a cabinet of family keepsakes. I wish I had had the presence of mind to take that box with me to the shipping container. (It angers me to think the paramilitaries might now have access to such personal items.)

I should add, too, that Stevie is greatly interested in birds. He waves "bye-bye" to birds, which more often than not are seagulls and crows. There are other birds he sees—Canada geese, blue herons, and Barrow's goldeneyes—but far fewer than the dominant species. I wish there was a greater variety of species close at hand. I would like Stevie to see a starfish in the wild. Or to eat a scallop or an oyster from our coast. But there are none. Acidification, low aragonite saturation, made the coast uninhabitable for shelled creatures. I studied it.

I also studied *adaptation*. For humans, that is. It is one thing—a sad thing—to lose the company of other creatures that evolved over millions of years, but quite another to fear for the survival of one's own offspring. To be sure, we are still quite far away from toxic concentrations of carbon dioxide (toxic for humans, that is). Nevertheless, I imagine a future in which the very rich drive around in sealed luxury cars—each with its own compressed air supply—while sickly servants asphyxiate outdoors.

To raise awareness of this possibility, I suggested, while brainstorming PR strategies for EcoRights, that we might ask, "Do you *breathe* oil?" I was referencing a question posed by Atahualpa, the last sovereign emperor of the Incas: noting his Spanish captors' obsession with gold, he asked them whether they ate it. Focus groups advised us against asking such a question. First of all, nobody would get the allusion. More importantly, *it wasn't polite.*

how I met my wife

About a month before my arrival in the compound, Yoshiko and I thought it would be a good time for her and Stevie to have an extended family visit in Japan—what with my job, and all the election-related lobbying I was doing. Now I wonder how much she knows of my circumstances. According to Janet, Yoshiko is aware I'm in a safety compound. I wrote her a letter for Janet to send through the post. A reply hasn't arrived yet, but it can't be easy to send one undetected. Surely it is only a matter of time. Yoshiko is the conscientious type, which is what attracted me to her in the first place.

She was in Canada on a working holiday visa when she visited our office, upstairs in an old brick tower on the edge of Gastown. She came in response to a call for volunteers. We needed people to deliver flyers around the city, help set up our tent at demonstrations, solicit donations, etc. In return they'd get meals and bus fare. Yoshiko wasn't so attuned to the lobbying dimension, but she knew about EcoRights through our *entry point activities*: cleaning up beaches and such. No one has a problem with that—not even our current government. It's the other stuff—the lobbying and press releases—that eventually got us (the Board and management) labeled *terrorists and insurrectionists*. And *pagan sorcerers* I believe, too.

It wasn't my intention to get Yoshiko messed up in these things. Nor was it my intention to keep her away from her home. Sometimes I feel sad that she gave up the life she had in Japan—proximity to her family, a career she'd just begun. She might have had a very different life if she hadn't met me. Perhaps an easier life.

It was just that she seemed *nice*, I wanted to see her without her clothes, and I couldn't *help myself*. She was in the habit of wearing tight jeans, which gave a strong impression of her tapered waistline. And she was small-chested, too—for some reason I've always been more turned on by small tits. She hardly ever wore a bra because she hardly needed one, and that was exciting, too. But there was more to my attraction than all that. I knew she was more to me than just another "junior tasty bite"— the term we had for a certain type of volunteer who came through our office. In any event, the fact is that I tried *very hard* to imagine what she would look like without her clothes. And I think any relationship leading to pregnancy, or even cohabitation, *must* start at that basic level.

silverfish

I am lonely without Yoshiko and little Stevie—not that I am entirely *alone*.

In my shipping container there are other living things, just as there were in my single days. Then, when asked how many there were in my household, I would deter telephone surveyors by reporting it was *hard to say*. There was me, and there were silverfish—but I couldn't say how many.

Now, as then, there are silverfish, and there are woodlice, too. Neither of these animals is a carrier of disease, so I am not worried they will harm me. If anything, they provide me with useful information: my dwelling is *too damp*. Simply, these creatures must live where it is damp and dark. If anything, they let me know to keep my lights on, and my door open when possible. (The silverfish scatter when, in daylight, I open the door suddenly.) If there is to be any harm arising from the presence of these animals, it is that they will eat my notepads. To prevent this from happening, I keep paper items sealed in a plastic bag, and as of yet have found no evidence of silverfish feeding on them. I am aware, though, that silverfish can live without food for up to a year, which is perhaps why I still find them around.

According to an erstwhile lover, woodlice—and by extension, silverfish—belong to a class of animals known as *the pathetic species*. These are animals that, in her words, "can die if you just look at them." At least they can be *killed* very easily—especially if they are stepped on. My insight, however, is this: such animals will not become *extinct* very easily. I see climate change having no adverse impact on these species.

This is a good thing because I can't imagine featuring such animals, if they were endangered, in promotional materials for EcoRights. It wouldn't elicit financial contributions. But I also can't see us putting humans in there, either. As humans, we're in control of our own destinies and are *invincible*—which does not reflect my view, of course. Nor that of Yoshiko, who, like me, *has a one child policy*.

not to be seen

Here I should clarify that I rarely leave my shipping container but for washroom breaks, or to queue up for food bank donations, which arrive two or three times a week in a one-ton truck. When outside, I avoid making eye contact, and speak to no one. This is to avoid detection.

Another way I avoid detection is to have no form of transceiver: no mobile telephone, no computer, no music player—nothing. It's because almost every such device these days is run with platform-specific software, difficult to hack, and impossible to run without authentication by an outside server. In other words, to operate one of these things you have to be watched. Even most radios these days are software-driven or integrated into some other kind of device. This is so the stations know how many listeners they have. But they can find out more, too. Janet is trying to get me some kind of old-fashioned radio.

Perhaps the authorities have already guessed I'm here. But as long as I'm here, out of contact, they may not care to track me down. Anyway, it's best not to take chances with my visibility—in case they're interested in more than simply having me off the grid. Janet says even if I encounter someone here who I think I can trust, not to discuss my circumstances directly, or reveal my name. There may be others here like me, but we need to protect one another by minimizing evidence.

Nevertheless, because I am so isolated, I am secretly hopeful to find a conversationalist, and my first opportunity seems to arrive one afternoon, as I sit in a portable toilet, admiring the patterned walls. As if in response to my most intimate, visceral sounds, I hear the metal lid of a nearby garbage can open and then close, bookending the clatter of bottles dropped inside. Next, I hear footsteps on damp earth. They approach my toilet stall, and a voice says: "KFNU9263743. KFNU9263743."

I attempt to memorize this apparent serial number because I think it is, perhaps, the address of an ally who knows of my presence.

another in the compound

When I find container 743 (finally, I figured it would suffice to remember just the last three digits), I knock.

"Is it you?"

"Yes."

As with most containers here, the lock rods have been removed, so I pull at the hasp-like mechanism at the door's opening edge. The door is heavy, and takes some effort to open and close.

"Please sit down."

Inside, the container is much like mine. The floor is soiled plywood. There is an air mattress and a sleeping bag, an oil radiator, and the same IKEA Kroby lamp. The occupant is a thin man with a beard—a beard that seems less an aspect of fashion than the consequence of personal hygiene being so inconvenient. (We have no warm running water, and the hairdressing students visit only every six weeks or so.) He wears thick-rimmed glasses, an orange, down-filled vest over a green, long-sleeved polypropylene undershirt, blue jeans, and soiled white tennis shoes. He has short hair, and his forehead is low and deeply lined. (I envy his hairline.)

"Would you like a cup of tea?" There is a plastic kettle unplugged from an extension cord.

"I'd like to know about that," I say, pointing to a poster above the sleeping bag on which the other man sits.

It is a photo diptych. On its left side is the famous Malcolm Browne image, in colour, depicting the self-immolation of Thich Quang Duc, the

Vietnamese monk. On the right is a cheery image of hot air balloons against a blue sky. The blue sky is not that far off from the colour of Duc's car, a 1956 Austin A95 Saloon. It is the car he drove to his self-immolation, and serves as backdrop to the scene. One of the hot air balloons is bright orange, the same colour as the flames in which Duc is consumed. The photographer of the hot air balloons is unknown (the photo was deemed not to have been as important), but the composer of the diptych is not.

"It's from an exhibit I saw in Toronto some years back. The artist—Hans Bielski—you might know of him."

"It's not an image I would expect to see hanging over someone's bed," I say.

"It's all I have for decoration."

"Can you tell me about the other images you saw there?"

"Not all of them."

"I don't want to hear about all of them—certainly not the Disneyland one."

my history as an artist

Hans Bielski is a pseudonym I've used whenever I've wanted to keep one part of my life separate from the others. I did the exhibit in Toronto, rather than Vancouver, to make doubly sure the Director of EcoRights (who uses my other name) was in no way implicated. For two weeks I rented a private gallery (now defunct) from a curator who told me he wanted to put on something "challenging." More likely he just wanted to make his rent. I believe the exhibit was seen by all of thirty people.

Perhaps I spent more time on the catalogue than on the exhibit itself. The catalogue extolled the artist, "Hans Bielski (19__ -), from Pissle, Germany," for embracing both "the documentary impulse" and "the ontological nature of the photograph." The show itself was described as "a disruption of anaesthetized social engagement" and "an exploration of ideological and aesthetic voids" unique for its "ambiguous intelligence" and its "hermeneutic." At the time I thought I was being necessarily clever. To a connoisseur, perhaps, my catalogue was equivalent to slipping on a banana peel in a comedy routine— which, to be fair to myself, isn't necessarily an embarrassment, depending on one's stage of removal. There are observations, observations of observations, and observations of those—though where the audience is at, no one can ever be completely sure. There were perhaps some who got nothing out of my show, and others quite a lot. 743 got something from it, apparently.

The title of the exhibit was *Reality Now*. Its main gimmick was a room containing a poster titled "Image Offensive to Most People." Entry to the room was restricted to visitors willing to disrobe completely—in order to "reciprocate the vulnerability of the artist."

working for an environmental agency

I always thought art had a place in social activism, and social activism in art. An early impulse—something that brought the two together for me—was a song by the singer Momus, "I Was a Maoist Intellectual," the crux of which is this:

I showed the people how they lived and told them it was bad

When I first got involved in the environmental movement, that's what I thought I needed to do, and it wasn't just a pop-song enticement. *I really meant it.*

Over time, however, activism became just a means to a living. My work for EcoRights wasn't what you'd call *activism*—it was an office management job, through which I earned higher than the median family income for the city in which I lived. This was justified as the *industry standard*. And why not? Why shouldn't I have been well remunerated for a job that exposed me to so many *desperate people*. Desperate because fund-raising consultants are a dime a dozen, and desperate because—let's face it—there's no secret to doing the work. You just have to be louder than everyone else.

And how did I rise in this line of work? By being sincere about it, at first. But mainly just by being around—and some cutthroat politics, because that's what it takes, and because I had no choice. That's because, for those with money, there's always money as a fallback. For the merely credentialed, like me, there are only positions.

hotels

There are also *junket trips*. As I wait here in my shipping container, I often remember the conferences I attended, and the hotels in which I stayed. Not *five-star* but usually in the *first-class* or *superior comfort* range. I can say they all had better pillows and linens than I could afford for my own home. And I remember:

> Water is vital in so many ways. Conserve water with one step. To use your towel again, place it on the rack. For a clean towel, place it on the floor.

If only I could use the same method here! Towel service is not available for my shipping container, though I wish it were. Even if I keep the heater on and leave the door open a crack, my towel smells mouldy after just a few days. There's nothing on which I can properly hang it, and there's insufficient light. Placing it on the floor would solve nothing, because there's no one to take it away. I can only wait until Janet or perhaps Dave or *someone* comes, so I can let them know what supplies I need, or ask them to take my mouldy towels and launder them somewhere. In the meantime, my only resource is a cold water tap—and the strength of my hands, to wring things out as thoroughly as I can. But it's not enough.

strategy

In the compound, as elsewhere, survival has always been my concern. For whichever reasons—perhaps it was my upbringing (if you believe in *intergenerational trauma*, though I won't get into that here)—I have always thought one must have *a clear strategy* for survival. One must always have a surplus of something, whether it is money, credentials, connections, or whatever. Or at the very least *a fallback plan*. A self-help guide, or a life coach might refer to these things as "capital." Of course I have never consulted a life coach, though I would agree most problems in life are a matter of degree. But there are also problems that can be answered only in binary terms, problems unmediated by an amount of something in reserve.

In politics it is unusual to attain a position *in perpetuity*, and there came a time, at EcoRights, when my instinct told me *something had to change*. Like many organisations, we were factional. The other faction—the old school, *founder's syndrome* faction (we referred to them as the "Blue Meanies")—had been resigned to letting us take the reins, but only for so long: they were waiting for a complacent moment (on the part of my faction, which we called "the progressives") to reengage their support. I saw all signs the moment was fast approaching, and that I had to shake things up—to reengage *the core radicals*—if we were to survive. (If I was to survive.) We called it "Ecology or Death." It probably sounds corny, that slogan. Wasn't Hugo Chavez its original author? Or is it owed to the Sandinistas? In any event—in retrospect—we were running out of ideas.

Audi S7 man

Here I return to the *man in the Audi S7*—or *AS7*, for short. I do so not only to emphasize that two very different realities can exist simultaneously, but also to emphasize a basic difference between us: that *survival* has never been a question for AS7. His only concern about survival is *how lavishly* he will do it. Again, I admit to having burned some fossil fuel, to having taken *a certain share* of expense accounts, of junket trips. For someone doing the hard work of saving the planet, a little comfort (just *superior comfort*, not even *five-star*) can be justified, can't it? But AS7 is a completely different story. No hotel, no restaurant, no flight—*nothing*—nothing is as elegant as that to which *he* has access.

Today, for example, he's on a flight from Vancouver to Tokyo, on Cathay Pacific. The Economy (that is, the government) needs to show some financial restraint, so he pays the difference for a First-Class Private Suite. He gets a down comforter, pyjamas, and a full selection of movies—even the Criterion Collection. (Will he watch *Ai no Corrida?*) And Cathay Pacific provides him with a fresh orchid, which is *a nice touch*. According to the company website, the First Class Private Suite provides "80% privacy." Not private enough to masturbate in the open, perhaps. But if he's paying this much, would anyone complain? It's unlikely they'd turn the plane back to Vancouver or make an emergency landing in Alaska.

In Tokyo he'll stay at the Shangri-la, where he'll get one of their six *super-luxury* suites with a private concierge. He'll ask the concierge to prepare him a list of entertainments, and he'll be shown flyers for all the traditional things: a *kabuki* performance, a *sumo* match, a temple visit.

"Sir, I recommend the 'Sora o Kizamu Mono,' at Kabuki-za."

"Yes, but I've seen that before. I'd like to see something more off the beaten path—not what all the tourists see."

The concierge shows him another set of flyers, including one for a basement club live performance by L'IMACE, a noise band on the Alchemy Records label.

"Is the club well ventilated?"

"I think you'll find lots of shoe smells in there, and not much lighting."

"How about something more intimate? I mean, that's intimate, what you just described. But, more, you know...."

Finally he'll settle for a two-hour haircut in Shinjuku, at a place called QS Hair Resort, where he'll be accompanied by an interpreter. The treatment will include a head, neck, and shoulder massage, and a choice of green teas. Afterward he'll stroll alone through Kabuki-cho. Who knows what he'll find there.

a haircut

I get a haircut, too. I'd already been a few weeks overdue when Janet evacuated me from my home, and it wasn't until some four weeks after my arrival that the students from the vocational college arrived to practise on *hair models*. Mainly it's about the school getting some cred as *a responsible corporate citizen*.

Someone knocks on my door in the morning and asks if I want my hair cut. An appointment is made at one of the communal-use locations, a white rental container. (As opposed to the abandoned or temporarily-out-of-circulation kind.) The barber's chairs are two old, mismatched bar stools with low seatbacks. The students have stepstools ready for height adjustments.

A shy and quiet boy is cleaning up the fringe of a balding man beside me, and my hairdresser is an equally reticent and *dull* young woman of twenty or so. But I shouldn't take her for dull just because she doesn't say much. What's there to ask someone who lives in a safety compound? Nor do I want to be asked.

The quiet boy has finished the man in the chair beside me. I can sense that this other *hair model* has noticed me. I can feel his eyes on me, as they say. And I predict he will do something—but I don't know what. Leaving, he interrupts the space between me and my hairdresser. He stands face-to-face with me, uncomfortably near. Prior to this I hadn't been able to get a close look at him, but now I notice something unusual about his face:

Two right eyes.

By which I do not mean two eyes on the *right side* of his face, but rather two right eyes. That is, when facing him, *the tear duct of each eye is on the right side*. It seems to have been achieved through some kind of plastic surgery.

"I can see that you are here," he says, and walks out.

a visit from Dave

I don't feel safe around anyone who has undergone extreme elective surgery. And I don't want to be seen here—especially not by someone with two right eyes. I'm not sure why I feel this way, but I think anyone with two right eyes is perhaps *not on my side*. That the man must be a spy. Or perhaps he has some *contagious mental ailment* that I, too, may catch. But how would that work?

"He's probably just some kook," says Dave. "I wouldn't worry about it. Lots of people are getting weird body modifications these days. And most of them are crazy. Face it: you're going to find lots of crazy people here. It's not just political refugees in these compounds. If he were a spy...would they hire a spy like that?"

I'm glad Dave is able to visit—by chance the day after the incident. He's arrived in the guise of a *bohemian tourist* or *flâneur*.

"Don't pay too much attention to what Janet says. It's in her nature to be cautious. I mean, you need to be cautious. Don't be stupid and start blabbing all over the place. But it's not going to do you any good if you're just worrying about getting tracked down. They just don't want you on the outside. That's all."

"Who?"

"You know."

"But there's that Sierra Club guy on indefinite house arrest. And the SofTorture™ and all that."

"Just put that out of your mind for a while, and leave the worrying to us. I've been studying up on shipping containers and how they're moved.

If we can find an 'in' down at the docks, maybe we can get you out of here, get someone to fabricate a new...something they call a high security seal."

"What's that?"

"I'm not exactly sure how all this stuff works—but just let us look into it. And try to get out a little bit. Wear a hat or something so you're not so recognizable. It's a pretty funky place, actually. There was a write-up about it in *Globe Style* recently. Like it's a cool place to hang out. *Local economy* and all that shit. Carnival stuff goin' on on the weekends. Just get out and walk around."

Before leaving he hands me a small wind-up radio and some headphones.

"Here's something to keep your mind off things. No software."

It's an Etón FRX1 from a few years back.

on air

Soon after Dave leaves, I connect to the FRX1 with the headphones he brought, and sit near the door to test the signal. The dial is highly sensitive. Moving forward through FM static I catch only a blip of what might be a radio station, then have to back up slowly, sometimes finding nothing. After some trying, I manage to land on a popular music station. I'm happy for the addition of noise—background static, and the tinny speaker, which seems perpetually overloaded. It adds to the sonic interest of the music, which in most cases is of no sonic interest at all—mostly preset sounds EQ'd the same way every time. I land on something like a sterilized send-up of Chic's "I Want Your Love," with a more direct message.

> The only way I'm gonna get through the day
> Is to screw like it's my last day
> I feel you penetrate my soul
> Gotta take your wand down below
> Gotta make your sweet, sweet magic come into me

These lyrics are quite typical for popular music nowadays. I believe the track is by Sweet Soul, the *romantic R&B* singer deemed innovative for *actually doing it* in one of her promo videos. I move on before the song reaches its chorus, if it even has one. (A lot of songs seem to have no refrain at all—at least not one that's noticeably catchy—and I wonder why they're so popular.)

Next on the dial is some kind of talk radio. They're asking *probing questions* about online combat games. *How extreme is too extreme? Should we be crowdsourcing military strikes? To what extent should we prevent gamers from hurting themselves?*

Just a few days ago, in Jerusalem, a Palestinian construction worker decided to visit a gaming arcade on his lunch break. While playing Krav Maga Extreme—a game developed by the Israeli Defense Forces—he inadvertently blew up his West Bank family home. In response to the incident, the IDF noted that all players have to sign an online liability waiver and that, although what happened is sad, the player "should have familiarized himself with local maps."

meditation on the shipping container

Back in the container—I estimate at least 90% of my time is *back in the container*—I have opportunities to examine its structure in detail. I can confirm it is not a filigreed castle, but perhaps one day it will be known for its *fine corrugation* and the *deliberate craftsmanship* of its welds.

Outside, as inside, it is a colour known as *dark spring green*. There were perhaps dozens—or even hundreds—of shipping containers manufactured to the exact specifications of the one in which I reside. Which is not to say any one of them lacks unique and accidental features.

Inside, facing the doors, I notice a spot at the top of the left wall, perhaps one third of the length of the wall from the doors, where the paint rises from the surface in the form of two drips, one slightly longer than the other. This is perhaps because, when the container was being painted, the spray nozzle was held either too close to or too long on that spot.

If paint has the same legendary properties as glass (a liquid that "drips" very slowly over years), these drips may still be dripping. If so, how long will it take for all the paint to drip off the walls? Or will the walls oxidize first? If I had a ruler, perhaps I could start measuring to verify over weeks, months, or years (please, let it not be years!) the velocity of this dripping paint.

Regardless of whether these drips are still moving or not, they are unique to this container—as is the shape of the welding bead. The welds here look very good, but there is no way they will look exactly the same from one container to the next. In this container I notice one or two spots where the bead is too wide, perhaps because the welder was momentarily distracted, scratching an itch, or responding to a coworker.

Likely the future will bring even more efficient construction techniques that leave no trace of human contact or hesitation. In that future, the design of the container in which I now reside will perhaps elicit nostalgia. Though to current sensibilities it seems generic, it may make way for something even more predictable and then be deemed to exemplify *a lost art*. Perhaps my container will be as different from the containers of the future as a baroque window frame is from those designed by Le Corbusier. Perhaps I am already feeling nostalgic for this place, not only because I can anticipate the future of industrial design, but also because I know that—*one day*—I will leave.

Because I am already feeling nostalgic for this container, I want to uncover its origins. I want to know who designed it. How much choice did they have in the profile of the corrugation? Or did they use a preformatted shape? If so, who designed that? I want to know where the shipping container was fabricated, the composition of its steel, and the area in which the materials were mined or collected. I want to go to the source—maybe a hole bored into the side of a mountain. Or a plantation of metal trees, somewhere in the Andes, where labourers pluck the metal fruit and place it in baskets. I want to meet the very man who cast his net into a cloud of metal needles. I want to meet the person—or people—who first connected with the source material. (If they are still alive.) Is this what is meant by *the furthest determinant*?

Janet visits

Janet is back. Rather, she is here for the first time, and brings a package of supplies, following a wishlist I sent with Dave. Among other things there is a small washbasin, a bottle of ammonia, plastic sandals, string and hooks, and a vaginal ointment.

"It says vaginal ointment, but according to my doctor it'll help for what you describe, and it's the strongest you can get without a prescription."

(When Dave was here I told him I had some kind of itch, in a sensitive area.)

"How'd you get here? I thought you said it was too risky for you to visit."

"The sandals are to wear in the bathing area—you don't want to get any more infections. Apparently they're building a sauna or a steam bath or something. So you might want to use that when it's done—to sweat some of the dirt out, if you don't want to stick with the sponge baths."

"And? News?"

"I'm here because we did a charity drive, so I'm delivering all the toiletries and socks we collected. Thought I'd see you while I'm here, too. LY's done a makeover of the organization. We're now going to be more charity-focused. She got the job as interim director."

"That psychotic bitch?"

"She's not that bad to work with."

"She's the reason I'm here. Going to the creeps about how she's so concerned we're being taken over by *radicals who don't have the best interests of the organization at heart*. And—"

"I know you see things a bit differently, but you have to trust that a lot of us are there working for you."

"So how did she end up being interim director? And how the fuck am I gonna get outta here? It's been—I don't know how many weeks—and I'm cold half the time, got hardly anything to read, now I've got some kind of infection, some guy with two right eyes is following me, my back is killing me, I'm eating from tins.... Could you at least get me something *fresh* to eat?"

"I put a few things in the bag over there. Some apples and a few zucchinis. I figured you could keep them around for a while."

"They'll be gone in a day. Sorry to be so ungrateful."

"Don't be. We're working on getting you out of here. You have to trust we're doing all we can."

"Heard from Yoshiko?"

"There's a letter from her in the bag. And I got you a few magazines, as well. One for if you need to relieve yourself—I hope you don't mind. I know that's a bit forward. Anyway, I think something called The Book Van is coming around in a few days or so."

AS7's mission

After Janet leaves, I read Yoshiko's letter. Apparently it's such a long time coming because she wanted to "save on postage." She asks if I have any "volunteers" with me in the compound. And then some advice: not to be too hard on myself. Still. But at least I know Stevie is all right. Yoshiko shows him my photo almost every day—so he doesn't forget his father.

I'll save my commentary on the letter for another time, because I recall now there is more to say about AS7. Honestly, I don't know that much about AS7 apart from my imaginings, which serve mainly to distract me from all the misery here. By which I mean the isolation, the cold, the infection, the packaged food, the filthy outhouses, cold water only, and the underwhelming concern I feel from those on the outside.

By contrast, AS7 lives a life of First Class Private Suites, posh hotels, expensive haircuts, guilt-free blow jobs by *volunteers* whenever and wherever, and other things. AS7 is, to use someone else's expression, practically *embalmed in money*. Curiously, he is not entirely a *bad guy*, whichever of those two words you choose to emphasize. Perhaps he is on my side. Or he is not on *their* side and he is doing some work that might help me, even if indirectly.

As you may have guessed, AS7 is on a diplomatic mission for the Economy. The Economy doesn't have diplomats any more—just business consultants—so his is a kind of on-call position. He's a philanthropist using his *soft power* to move things in less of a bad direction. He is able to negotiate and *understand both sides*, a Liberal Democrat type. He was appointed by the Conservatives as a *nice gesture* to plural politics. He does it simply to *bear witness* (his term for it) because he doesn't really need the money. He's on some kind of parliamentary economic rights (formerly human rights) committee.

But can he find a *reasonable solution* to my problem? Maybe he's asking whether economic criminals in one country might be accepted elsewhere where they aren't criminals, in exchange for something. He feels for people like me. It goes roughly like that. He thinks that deep down each and every one of us can be *reasonable* and find a *reasonable solution* to our problems. Our politicians are *reasonable people*, after all, responding only to the *democratic will*. Something like that.

the risks

So, what would happen if I got impatient and couldn't wait for my comrades, or AS7, or whoever, to find a *reasonable solution*—or even a *clandestine solution*—to get me out of here? Before I answer that question, here's an excerpt (reproduced as best I can remember it) from a recent position statement issued by the Economy:

> For over two hundred years, our Economy has functioned to protect us from terrorism committed by those who would deny us the right to jobs, money, and freedom. Our Economy was founded on anti-terrorism, and to deny the existence of terrorism—as some have done—is to deny the existence of our Economy, and is an act of sedition.

For my part, I suggested publicly that a protester putting himself in the way of a bulldozer was not a *terrorist*, but rather someone committing an act of civil disobedience. This was a matter of public contention a few months before the election. Contentious enough to send me to a term in prison—as just one potential outcome. Or held indefinitely on a Security Certificate. Or interrogated using SofTorture™, to determine whether there were allegations against me, and whether those allegations needed to be tested in court. To be fair to the Economy, I can at least be assured all would be done according to *legal processes*. Regardless, my options are unattractive—and for that reason I am careful.

shiatsu

After reviewing the above, I believe I need to be more specific. The real problem is the Economy, and they need to be more specific, too. Of course they do. More specific than SofTorture™—though I don't want to describe here what it really means. But I need to be clearer about what happened with the bulldozer—to be clear about what "putting himself in the way" really means. It means that *some guy*—he wasn't even an Ec-oRights member—put a land mine (it's incredible what you can buy on-line today) in the way of the bulldozer. To be fair, he had left a "warning box," Squamish Five-style, at the foreman's office. It had a countdown timer, a stick of dynamite, and a note letting the work crew know what was there. But the crew kept working anyway—and one of them got hurt. And the note made reference to "Ecology or Death."

Politically, it could have played out in all sorts of ways. But as *core radicals* are apt to think, the times are a-changin', and pretty soon everyone is going to see what a sham system we have and rise up to make it end, to replace it with something *better*. And rise up they did—in the form of a "text field revolution" (I came up with that myself). Online donations were rolling in steadily, as were messages of support. The Conservatives spoke to their base, too, modified their election platform with a pledge to include "shareholders" as an "identifiable group" under the hate propaganda sections of the Criminal Code. So I got some hate from them, but mostly all sorts of e-mails and FaceWatch messages encouraging me to "hang in there," thanking EcoRights for "forefronting" the environment in our "national debate," and such. The "Ecology or

Death" campaign seemed to be having its intended impact: highlighting the importance of the environment, highlighting the unreasonableness of our government. But at the end of the day—at the end of each day monitoring online support—I was the only one left in the office. And, because I had been alone before in my life, I knew I was alone then, too: I felt the vertigo. I think I knew my support just wasn't that deep. That the only real "capital" I had left was Yoshiko and little Stevie.

At home I tried to stay as cheerful as I could—to be Stevie's papa as well as I could, not wanting to pass down the *intergenerational trauma*, because I believe such a thing is possible. But I was living in fear of what might happen, performing all other parts of my life without feeling, and regretting it.

At such times—when we were alone, after we had put Stevie to bed—Yoshiko would take one of my hands in both of hers, massage the palm, stretch the fingers, press between the thumb and index finger. Without looking up she would say: "You're not alone, you know."

It was at such times that I really noticed Yoshiko—as someone completely generous to me. And I think that way about her now, too. She's the only one I could really always count on. Can really always count on, despite my "volunteers" and all, I'm sure.

Which is why there must be a home and a life for me in Japan.

outliers

Here, in the meantime, is a life that rather keeps me out of the open. And yet I build, gradually, on my impressions of the place, on my knowledge of those who are here with me. Now I know something of 743, and there are others, too, about whom I know nearly as much—simply through glimpses I receive during my daily routine.

Not all here are housed in shipping containers. There is, for example, a neo-hippie couple who live in a white, late 1980s Volkswagen T3 van. I'm sure they would have preferred an earlier T2 in a brighter colour, but the important thing is it's a VW van. He is skinny, clean-shaven, and has straight, shoulder-length dark hair. She is not so skinny, but not fat either, and often wears a peasant dress. They have a fair-complexioned daughter with Down syndrome. She is perhaps seven or eight years old. The father plays guitar—he has a wide repertoire, and I suspect he may once have tried seriously to make it as a musician. The mother has a sandwich board outside the van, and it reads:

HEALING PRACTISES (rates negotiable):
- yoga
- past life regression
- loving kindness meditation
- mother and infant acupuncture

Elsewhere, far from the family with the van, there is a young man with a long beard, and he seems always to be meditating. There are also small-time drug dealers (who look much like one would expect), and I have occasionally seen a pale, shirtless punk-rock woman in tight, ripped jeans. She has her hair in the Chelsea style, and for modesty wears standard black electrical tape Xs over her nipples. She also wears a leather jacket with the following inscription on its back panel:

```
            I
            L
    M K U L T R A
            U
            M
            I
            N
            A
            T
            I
```

Elsewhere in the compound, someone has decorated their container with Canadian flags, and when I have to go out, I make sure not to go near it: on principle, I avoid people showing strong signs of mental illness. I have compassion for them, to be sure, and I realize no one is precisely on the median of mental health. But when I encounter someone who is *deeply ill*, I don't want to be anywhere around them. It's just the way I feel.

burning boat

From time to time I've felt guilty or wrong in my quickness to dismiss what I don't understand, and that feeling seems to motivate a recurring dream of late. The dream concerns a burning boat, and a sense of having caused it to burn myself; also that I was wrong to set the boat on fire, and that the event has *meaning*. But that's not what impresses me most about the dream. Symbolism in dreams is hardly unexpected. Rather, it's that the setting and main event are so *uncannily real*, like memories of a true experience, yet vague and paradoxical.

The dream has a strangely familiar geographic location—a sheltered cove, specific yet unnameable, with evergreen trees in a cool climate. There the boat burns with a steady roar. Orange cinders stand out against grey-black smoke in the late afternoon light. They drift to the water in a slight breeze, hiss upon contact.

The boat itself is an archetype—a boat with masts, anachronistic—and yet I feel it's from the future, from as far away as another planet or a supernatural realm. Though it shouldn't be large if set against my knowledge of boats, it makes a large impression—as if it is a *ship* rather than merely a *boat*. These contradictions unsettle me. They make me feel like the unwilling taker of a strange and sinister cognitive association test.

Moreover, someone is with me in the dream—someone familiar, but whose face I can't recall. The only clear detail is her voice.

She says: "I wonder if that was the right thing to do."

I say: "I don't know."

the book van

One of the charities that regularly visits the compound is called The Book Van. Members of this charity believe we all shall be redeemed through books, so they drive from location to location with a portable library. The library is housed inside a high-ceilinged Mercedes-Benz Sprinter van (white, of course), fitted with bookshelves along each of its side walls. The books are held in place with elastic cords.

Few of the books are precious—most are paperback novels with shiny covers, often with raised foil lettering to highlight titles such as *Crash!*, *Plot of Terrors*, *Windswept*, *486*, *Lost in the Woods*, *Clash of the Galaxies*, *The Sardinian Lover*, *The Ktoth Conspiracy*, *Destiny*, *The Purple Corset (Part Three in The Trilogy of Dhong)*, and such like. There are also books of a more practical nature (*How to Make Twig Furniture*), and on my very first visit to The Book Van I find something called *The Anxiety Workbook*. Although I am invited to borrow this book without ID—or just keep it—I choose to read it in the van and return it to the shelf. Little in it is terribly memorable, although the following passage stands out:

> Susan awakens suddenly almost every night, a couple of hours after going to sleep, with a tightness in her throat, a racing heart, dizziness, and a fear that she's going to die. Although she's shaking all over, she hasn't a clue why.

It prompts me to examine what is meant by "a tightness in her throat." That is, what would it mean simply to have "a tight throat"?

Normally, when we talk about these things, aren't we more direct, or at least nonspecific? That is, are there different kinds of tightness and is Susan having trouble defining which one? Is it moist tightness? Dry tightness? For comparison, do I get a *soreness* of my back, or a *hardness* of my penis? (Often, and hardly ever now.) And with this discovery (of the discourse, that is), I find the key to my stylistic objection! Here the soreness and hardness are the subjects, so to speak, of the predicative clauses. If I were to say my back is sore or my penis is hard, it is the body part at the centre, rather than the sensation. Of course, neither body part is truly the subject of the *sentence*. That would be "I." So this passage, despite its inclusion in an apparently inconsequential book, has opened for me a truth: that is, it is not the *thing* that matters, but the *feeling*.

bowl of dirt, a manta ray

The morning after my first visit to The Book Van I find a bowl of dirt just outside the door of my shipping container, close enough to make me feel it was left intentionally. The bowl is like a bowl one might see in a gold rush museum—which is not to say it is like a gold pan. It looks like mass-produced china might have in the nineteenth century, something found in an abandoned frontier house. The dirt is fine, seemingly sterilized, the kind of soil one might purchase at a nursery.

Later the same day, returning from an errand, I happen to pass by a shipping container in front of which a man, with his back turned to me, is standing before a tabletop mounted on sawhorses. As I approach, I notice something like a small ray or a skate on the table—perhaps a model of a ray or skate, or one prepared by a taxidermist. On closer inspection it seems to be a starry skate (*raja stellata*), and I notice the man is attempting to glue a pair of juvenile deer antlers to its back. As I pass he turns to me and says, in a gentle voice, as if teaching a new word to a small child: "It's a manta ray," with a strong emphasis on *manta*. Then he says: "I will grow it in the soil."

It is the man with two right eyes.

a tapir?

On the topic of nature, I am reminded of the animal I saw—the one that was cornered by the toughs and their girlfriend. What kind of animals do I know that are native to this area and fit the same profile? The answer is none. The only animal to match the profile would be a tapir. A mountain tapir, perhaps. Come to think of it, didn't I hear something about moving them from the Andes to be preserved elsewhere? And there was something, too, in a recent newspaper science section. Something about mating them with woolly mammoths, to "preserve the genetic heritage" of each—*because it can be done and therefore should be done*.

If it is a tapir, I wonder who brought it here, and what they plan to do with it.

the governor of Tokyo

Now is perhaps a good time to return again to AS7, currently in Japan.

He is having an audience with a former Governor of Tokyo, a man of influence. The meeting takes place at the former Governor's penthouse apartment, in Tokyo's Akasaka district, conveniently located within walking distance of the Canadian Embassy, which has been remodeled as The Canadian Natural Resource Museum funded by oil, gas, and mining corporations, not all of which are Canadian. The current exhibit is titled "The Cowboy and the Samurai—at One with Nature." The diplomatic functions of the Embassy are minimal, but the Diplomatic Coordinator, despite his tiny office, has connections: he can be credited with arranging this meeting, and providing AS7 with an interpreter—a shy, somewhat plump young woman dressed in what to the unacquainted might seem like fetishwear—in fact the standard uniform of a Japanese office lady, or *OL*.

The former Governor's penthouse is located in a surprisingly tall (for the area) white tile apartment building with a small, utilitarian lobby occupied by an expressionless, white-gloved concierge of a certain (post-retirement) age. Arriving at the penthouse suite, AS7 and his interpreter are greeted by the former Governor himself, who wears a *yukata* and slippers. Standing meekly behind him at the door is a former Prime Minister of the United Kingdom, with whom the former Governor cohabits.

After removing their shoes, AS7 and his interpreter are taken to the expansive living room. On the interior side of this room, the former Governor and AS7 sit across from one another at an angular oak bar. A white-gloved butler serves sake along with a number of small tripe dishes, and the former Prime Minister of the United Kingdom retreats to a leather sectional sofa close to the tinted wall-to-ceiling windows. He works on a laptop computer. It is the middle of a bright yet overcast day, but in the room it feels like early evening, and the bar is illuminated with a spotlight.

Beyond initial greetings, AS7 and the former Governor proceed with the following conversation, as mediated by the interpreter:

"This is a very impressive view."

"This is cow guts—*man food*. Do you eat cow guts in Canada?"

"The hors d'oeuvres are very good."

"You should not speak French. The numbers don't make sense. What the hell is *quatre-vingts*?"

"I come from the English part of Canada."

"Is that right? I suppose that's fine, then. The British are fine. Japan and Great Britain are both island countries. Do you have the four seasons in Canada?"

"We have spring, summer, winter, and fall. Winter is very cold, but now it's getting warmer, so it's more comfortable."

"That's good. The British like a mild winter."

"I very much admire Japan, and I have wanted to meet you for a long time. Your inspiration, Mishima Yukio—I like his story, 'Patriotism.'"

"You know Mishima Yukio?"

"Yes."

"Really! And do you know Japanese *sake*? Is it strange to you?"

"No, it is very good. This is very fine *sake*."

"It is Watari Bune. The best. I'm glad you like it. You're not just some stupid asshole foreigner."

"Thank you."

"In the story, 'Patriotism,' the woman is fine. Women are, generally speaking, stupid. But one with equal resolve.... The woman, like the one in 'Patriotism,' who will follow her husband to death with equal resolve. She is good. Do you like Japanese women?"

"Yes, of course."

(The interpreter blushes and averts her gaze.)

"Let me show you something."

The former Governor asks his butler to present a certain short film, on a flat screen adjacent to the bar. In this film, two young women remove their clothes and a team of mostly male makeup artists cover their bodies in cheetah camouflage markings. Following this, the young women crawl on all fours through a room of potted plants. They make meowing noises and chase one another.

"Do you have women like that in Scotland?"

"Not exactly like that, but very close. That was a very impressive performance."

"They are the best."

"Now, if it's okay, I want to talk about our treaties. The one about refugees and what is not a crime in my country is a crime in yours and what is a crime in mine is not a crime in yours, and maybe we can do an exchange. We can have equal grace. Equal resolve. We have some environmental terrorists and you have some...."

"You understand us well. To get rid of.... Like in the story 'Patriotism,' we put down our knives before us with equal resolve. In this way."

"It is the way."

"Mishima.... He was a true man. I want you to tell everyone in France, or wherever you're from, that he was a true man."

"I can certainly do that."

Quatre-vingts!

As the meeting concludes, the former Governor, visibly drunk, rises abruptly to guide AS7 to the door. As he stands up to leave, AS7 notices that the former Prime Minister of the United Kingdom now has his pants unbuttoned and is wiggling his soft penis frantically with one hand, while navigating an online game of Krav Maga Extreme with the other. Noticing he is being watched, the former Prime Minister of the United Kingdom turns to AS7, smiles shyly, and makes a loud, breathy exhalation.

The former Governor says: "Don't worry. I understand your feeling." It is not clear, however, to whom this is addressed, or to what it refers. Nevertheless, AS7 feels that his point has been made and that his proposal will be a success. It is, of course, just a *feeling*. He won't know for sure until something is signed. Either way, he understands not to push the matter.

music in the compound

Beyond made-up stories, it has been a habit of mine to find distraction in music. In the compound, however, music is sparse. I am not fond of what I hear on the few stations received by the FRX-1 and have stopped using it. On occasion, the failed rocker will sit on a plastic milk crate outside his VW van, covering a song or two by The Escalators ("The Day the Sun Burned Down") or The Chameleons ("View from a Hill"). This is acceptable to me, but the arts charities have dubious taste. They once brought us *a West Coast folk singer-songwriter*, who sang something about "waitin' for a revolution." He sang it with a strong southern-US drawl, even though he didn't *speak* with such an accent.

In any event, while it is somehow curious that music should be so rare in the compound, it is perhaps not *a bad thing*. After all, the prevailing mode is still the same old crap, as it has been for decades. In *The Globe and Mail*, I read the review of an album deemed *a crossover success*, equally popular with "teenagers, middle-aged men driving luxury brand cars, humourless career women on fertility drugs, liberal politicians, William Gibson, and medical lab technicians smearing shit on glass slides."

the police

Returning from the food truck one morning (with a variety of tins in a barely adequate plastic bag), I encounter two of the young men who had cornered the tapir. They are standing at the door end of a container and are being questioned by three police officers. The cops are all in their 30s, dressed in black body armour, with billy clubs and stun guns on their belts.

I've just rounded a corner into one of the container alleys. Thinking it would look suspicious to turn back, I instead keep walking toward the group, hoping to pass undetected. Getting closer, I hear the conversation that's in progress, but the words aren't clear. And then one of the young men is on the ground, and one of the cops is on top of him, his knees on the man's neck and shoulders, grabbing an arm and pulling it violently back. The other young man bolts, and one of the cops gives chase.

"Hold off!" says the third cop, apparently the crew leader. "We know where to find him."

The cop who ran off returns, and at this point I'm almost at the scene. I keep walking. I believe it would look natural to keep walking.

"Are you resisting?" asks the leader.

(Unclear mumbling.)

"He seems to be resisting," says the cop on top of the young man.

"Stop resisting!" It's the other cop, clearly pissed at not being able to run down the escapee.

"Okay, then," says the leader, reaching for his stun gun.

"I'm not!" yells the young man.

Now I'm directly at the scene and the clearly pissed cop turns to me. "Keep moving. Nothing to see."

I keep moving, without looking back.

"Don't. Please." It's the muffled voice of the young man. Following this is silence—it might be only a few seconds, but it seems longer. Then I hear something thud, or crack—a sound I have never heard before.

words

Now the burning boat is back—or just its location. The same dream location, not far from the evergreen cove. With the same woman, too. Beside me in my peripheral vision. I have a strong feeling we are alone—or more correctly, abandoned.

"You were naïve," she says.

I say nothing.

"Why did you think they would stay in their world? There's just one world, you know."

"They were going to do what they were going to do, no matter what I thought. We know it now. We didn't know it then."

"You need to find a way to remember."

"I will."

The words in this conversation are distinct—I can remember every single one of them. The context, though, is unclear. Less than unclear. Who are "they" and what did they do?

Despite its lack of clarity, the conversation has a resonance for me: a Danish film I saw some years ago. I've forgotten all the details, but in the film a politician gives a speech. Mid-speech, a car thief asks to borrow the politician's keys—ostensibly because the politician's car is blocking an exit route. In *a grand gesture*, he tosses his keys to the thief and says to his audience: "If we don't have trust, *what do we have?*"

another conversation with 743

I am back at 743's container, without an appointment. I knock and start to pull at the heavy door. I get it open enough to enter sideways, but before I make it through, he already has a suggestion.

"I see you're here for your reading! Your tarot card reading," he says, gesturing to the upper corners of his container box, as if to tell me we aren't alone. "Today I'm sure you have many questions, and it's best to touch them through a barrier."

I pause, think, and decide it's best to play on his terms. "You mean it's best not to test too hard. Is that what you mean?" I ask.

"Only that the test is hard, so I'm putting out a sign."

"Like a sandwich board."

"Yes! To board a boat. Board of directors. Sandwich board. Advertising for clients. Before it was only word of mouth."

"Word of mouth."

"And not the same meaning as today or tomorrow or yesterday."

"But you know who's guarding the gate." This is perhaps my main interest.

"A gate that's never open and never shut."

"You mean I can leave anytime."

"You can, but it's best to wait for the preparations I've heard about from no one."

"What about right eyes?"

"That's not a part of our conversation, and perhaps not a part of the others'. Nobody knows."

"And past life regression?"

"Harmless, but perhaps worthwhile. Getting back to the eyes, though— yours or those of another—there's something you should know."

I wait for him to continue.

"It might alarm you if something appears but does not mean."

"Or it might embarrass me. For investing in nothing, if it means nothing."

"Or you could see it like this: simply that you haven't reached the limit of what you can know about it. Like a glove, painted with the anatomy of nerves, lined with fragments of glass."

"How so?"

"In no way at all."

"I see."

"Do you? To make double sure, I want to be clear: I don't mean not to beware."

"Now is perhaps not the best time." I mirror his hand gesture around the top corners of the container.

"We'll continue this reading later," he says.

family day in the compound

National Family Day is a midwinter holiday. Most of us inside the compound don't really need a day off—not in the usual sense of *a day off work*. Nevertheless, a charity group has decided to provide us with a little enjoyment—a little reprieve from the routine, if indeed we have a routine. They have provided a large screen on which we are to view the Prime Minister's National Family Day Address—to help us feel that we, too, are *part of the family*.

The cost of this event is likely quite low: I notice the screen and sound system have been supplied by a company called Town Squire. Their business model is advertising: advertisers pay to have their messages displayed on the screen. From nearby telephones and other transceivers, a receiver collects FaceWatch data, and between main events displays advertisements on the screen, selected based on prevailing audience interests.

Perhaps due to the lack of data here in the Compound (few of us have mobile telephones), the advertisements seem not to follow any particular theme. We see promotions for semiconductors, a hamburger restaurant chain in another province, a car called the Infiniti Landscape Grandé Ultra, a cluster bomb dispenser, and a masturbation/sperm-storage device for "the busy executive" based on "the ancient Indian ritual practise of *sum-bhog*, and the Japanese concept of *kaizen*."

Immediately prior to the Prime Minister's speech, we see a short film about Canada, in which the country is shown to be *a land of opportunity*—a male voice-over tells us so. Hearing this vocal performance, I recall the story (uncorroborated) that Giorgio Moroder gave Donna Summer some *encouragement* for the recording of "Love to Love You." In the case of this film, however, there is little doubt the narrator is getting *real stimulation*.

Inter-spliced with aerial views of a vast landscape, we see young men Jet Skiing on a summer lake, getting their machines fueled up by young women wearing gas station "uniforms": translucent pink bikinis. Businessmen shake hands in front of a pipeline. A hockey player pushes another to the ground and beats him with his stick. At a circus, a performer in a fireproof suit douses himself with gasoline and lights himself on fire as children look on in wonder. Two cowboys are served beer from a modified gas-pump nozzle by a busty bartender wearing a half-top with "BURST" written across it. Soldiers perform SofTorture™ on a terrorist. A romantic couple embrace as they watch the sun go down, reflected on a tailings pond. Cut to: oil gushing suddenly from the end of a flexible hose. A pompous martial soundtrack subsides, and we arrive at the Prime Minister's National Family Day Address.

The Prime Minister tells us how "deeply honoured" he is to address his "countrymen and -women." He lets us know he really means *every single one of us*, "from the brave soldiers who defend us from economic terrorists, to the hard-working bankers who invest in our communities." And he extols our national character—one of hardy, go-getter independence. We learn, for example, about the sisters who succeeded in raising enough money for their uncle's heart surgery—by way of an intimate calendar. Now they're doing a cross-country tour called "Spread Love Wide for Max Provide," teaching others how to raise funds.

I watch this performance from the slightly parted door of my shipping container. The crowd is sparse, and the response is muted. No one applauds, but no one heckles, either—I think because they are being watched. (But not because they are being watched by me.) There might be other reasons for this reticence, but I can't be sure.

the Tokugawa period

Here I should give more credit to The Book Van, which also takes part in the Family Day celebrations. I discover they still don't carry any of my former textbooks—such as *Coastal Engineering* or *Air Pollution Emission Factors*—but this time I notice, hopefully, a number of more serious titles. For example, books on history—a topic that interests me lately. From a table in a book called *A History of Japan: From Early Modern to Postmodern*, I learn about "key values and practises in the Tokugawa period" including:

- widespread orthodoxy and conformism
- widespread obedience—at least in form—to authority, and an idea of "freedom within limits"
- continued distinction between formal authority and actual power, and by extension between outer form and inner substance
- continued preference for equating "wrong" with disruption and disobedience rather than evil
- "morally relaxed" attitude towards sexuality
- collective responsibility and accountability enforced by vigilance and harsh punishment
- cautiousness towards strangers with strong in-group / out-group consciousness
- sense of materialism
- continuing view that life is relatively cheap
- a strengthening sense of nationalism

Constitution of the Economy of Canada

As another historical note, in 20– the Canadian Charter of Rights and Freedoms was replaced with a simplified, one-page document, titled The Constitution of the Economy of Canada. Apart from the title, the Prime Minister's signature, and the date on which the document was signed, it consists merely of a single sentence, introducing "the founding principles of our nation":

HARD WORK

MONEY

FREEDOM

PART TWO

... what I regard as the objective, more or less deliberate manifestations of my existence are merely the premises, within the limits of this existence, of an activity whose true extent is quite unknown to me.

ANDRÉ BRETON, *NADJA*

I dream of an oceanside forest of spruce and pine rising from an almost continuous layer of salal bushes. Just beyond, thin light sparkles on a calm inlet. The light seems as if filtered through a layer of frosted glass. The air temperature is cool, but it must be summer because the salal berries are ripe. There are thimbleberry bushes and salmonberries, too—the former also in season. The shrubs are separated in a few places by narrow trails littered with driftwood. Common Witch's Hair—a kind of lichen—flows from branches.

I am with a young woman, and I seem to be young, too. She carries a woven basket and is pinching off salal berries, placing them inside. Perhaps I am doing the same thing, but I am far more attentive to her than to the task. I notice certain details: her black hair, braided, her fingers, brown and delicate, her breasts, suggested by the way her shawl hangs on her chest. She speaks to me in an unfamiliar language, and yet I know what she says:

"We're going to be together for a long time, eh?"

There's a feeling between us, on the edge between modesty and pride. It might boil over, merge with the obscene. The feeling is strong enough to have its own colour. I am a part of that colour, and I keep seeing it for many days after I have this dream. It makes me want to cry. I want to go back because it seems like a true memory.

What else could it be?

the ocean container

All of my dreams and most of my thoughts happen inside my shipping container—to such an extent I've started calling it an *ocean container*. Intermodal shipping containers are often referred to as such—in the sense they are containers taken across oceans. But I am not referring to something on the surface of the sea, but something deep within it, and a sense of limitlessness.

There are few distractions inside this ocean container. So when I think and dream, I become so consumed with my feelings that even the world beyond the container—when I enter it—is endowed with them. It's like spending days on end at a film festival, seeing so many movies they seem to continue into the street upon leaving the theatre. Gradually, in just the way film creates a feedback loop with the non-film world, I start to see more of my thoughts and dreams reflected beyond my container.

Here I want to assure you I'm not delusional: I am fully capable of telling the difference between what is within me and what is without. It's just that now—thanks to my concentration, my isolation—my boundaries have altered. I see the world in a different way, perhaps a more perceptive way, through different insights.

To be clear, I still take inspiration from the external world. Indeed, I am feeling more off guard outside the container—and there are reasons to go outside.

noh theatre

A theatrical society, a group with a mandate "to increase awareness of Japanese arts" (although they don't say why it is important or even necessary to do so), has announced a series of performances called *Edo: Pleasure District in the 21st Century*. There are posters all over the compound. The performances—rather a series of dress rehearsals prior to a tour of major cities—will be free to all residents, and are scheduled under the cover of night, giving me confidence to attend: darkness makes it easier to blend in.

Some of the performances are more like workshops or lectures, and at the first of these I keep a low profile toward the back of the seating area. We sit on the ground, on plastic tarps. We are outside in our warmest clothes. Bamboo torches provide light, and the performers speak to us from a portable folding stage, perhaps half a metre off the ground. A four-panel *byōbu* screen serves as a backdrop. It's a half-size screen, like a 1:2 scale model, predominantly gold with a misty mountain vista. (It looks like the *byōbu* I once found at a yard sale: I went away to consider whether I really needed it, decided I did, and came back to find it had already been sold. Is there a word for such experiences?)

There are three performers, and the leader of the group is a tall, elderly man. He wears a kind of *kimono*, and a *Noh* mask—a pale, expressionless mask that's far too small for his face. Tonight's lecture is about *Noh* theatre.

"Tonight, as we introduce the form and origins of *Noh*, we will perform an abbreviated *Noh* play," he says. "Unusual for *Noh*, our group performs a hybrid of *Genzai* and *Mugen Noh*, combining subject matter of the present, linear, and so-called 'real' world with that of the supernatural."

The group leader presents the performance roles on a signboard, stage right:

SHITE: the main protagonist
WAKI: foil for the protagonist
TSURE: companion of the protagonist

"The *tsure*, which is my role, sometimes removes himself from the action to address the audience directly, with commentary or explanation."

Two passersby—young guys, perhaps the same I saw corner the tapir—comment on the signboard: "Hey. They're going to do some shite acting."

"*Shite*. That's \she-tay\," says the group leader.

a final visit

It's early afternoon on a cold, dry day, and I'm in my sleeping bag, taking a nap. The oil-filled radiator is on full blast. It always has to be. There's a tinny rap at the door, and someone asks for me by name. It's Dave. Today he's wearing a pair of glasses I haven't seen on him before. A pair of updated brow-line glasses. Titanium, perhaps. I say they look expensive, ask if he's scammed the benefits plan.

"These? I've had them for a couple of months now. Guess we haven't seen each other in a while. Or maybe I wasn't wearing them last time."

Dave doesn't seem his regular, jovial self, and the glasses don't help. The whole Malcolm X look—by which I mean brow-line glasses—never gives the impression one's just *joking around*.

"I've brought this for you," he says, indicating a duffel bag set down by the door.

I look inside: soap, toothpaste, and a brush. Canned soup, cauliflower, a small propane burner with a couple of canisters, a twelve-pack of toilet paper. An aluminum pot, cash, and some other things.

"I've been wanting to heat up my own food. Thanks. Nothing more from Yoshiko?"

"Whatever Janet gave me for you is in there."

"Anything about getting me out?"

"Not a lot."

"What's going on?"

"Janet's been kinda silent lately. Says she's working on things, trying to suss out some options with the rail workers. Honestly I'm finding it hard to make a connection with her—I guess things are busy in the office. The idea is to get you on a sealed container straight from here. One we know isn't gonna get opened."

"Any progress at the docks?"

"Seems people are gutless about smuggling these days. I know a few who've done the old Kootenay trails, but there's not much use in you crossing the border. There's someone who says he might knock off a security seal, but it's kinda sketchy. Then we need to know which numbers are going where, what kind of supplies you need. I don't think it's gonna happen soon."

"I could just walk out of here."

"I wouldn't do that. And anyway, you don't have your ID."

"Why don't you bring it to me?"

"What if they do a search? Anyway, it's getting easier to stay here, you know."

"Yeah?"

"I hear someone's trying to make a sauna and a shower room."

"Oh."

"We'll keep bringing you supplies—but I need to tell you this is probably my last visit. Janet thinks we're close to getting tailed. If we aren't already. But we've got a connection here, so—"

"Is he the one—"

"I don't know who. Not supposed to know. I don't have all the answers at this point."

do they or don't they?

I imagine someone who *does* have all the answers, or at least the ability to find them: AS7. I imagine he's waiting for a train at Tokyo Station. He's on his way to Kyoto to visit Gion Shinbashi, which is or *was* another kind of walled compound, a real pleasure district, or a *Disneyland* pleasure district. No one knows for sure. In any event, it'll be a treat to himself before returning home.

The bullet train from Tokyo to Kyoto is two hours. AS7 has reserved a private compartment and plans to consume at least four cans of Kirin grapefruit *Chu-Hi* on the way. That's a drink every half hour, and he's purchased an extra two just in case. He likes Kirin *Chu-Hi* because it's fizzy and not too light in alcohol—even though it's cheap. His compartment is on the north side of the train, so he can see Mt. Fuji. Once he's done that he'll prepare for arrival by reading a guidebook to Gion. He'll read about the *Kanikakuni* commemorating poet Isamu Yoshii, but he'll hardly care. Instead he'll be thinking about any number of *shunga* prints: a cartoon vulva, penetrated in an Utamaro woodblock (something he saw on a trip to the British Museum) or Hokusai's *Dream of the Fisherman's Wife*—the coital scene of a woman and two octopodes.

In Gion, with the help of a discreet translator, he'll choose one teahouse among others with latticed doors and windows. Perhaps the girls will be lined up in their hand-painted *kimonos*. How will he choose?

"You had better choose carefully," his interpreter will say, conveying the advice of a teahouse *mama-san*. "Admire their subtle beauty. Observe the powdered napes of their necks."

After his choice is made, he might bathe in a teahouse *sentō*, arrive refreshed to a private *tatami* room where *sake* will be poured by his chosen *geisha*—or will she be a *maiko*? Never mind. She will play a tune on the *shamisen*, and his penis will start to quiver under the only layer he wears: a cotton bathrobe. It's not easy to control these things when one is tired and hung over, and he'll wonder if it's rude to harden visibly in her presence.

When the song reaches its end, so might the *geisha's* performance. She might leave the room, or continue to the next stage, and the next. Perhaps she'll unwind her *obi*—if she can. If it's not just the shape of an *obi*. Here I'm thinking of Stanislaw Lem's *Solaris*, or the scene in the Tarkovsky film, the one in which Kris tries to take off Hari's clothes. Hari is just a simulacrum and so is her dress, the fastener a two-dimensional imitation. Kris has to cut it off with a pair of scissors. Will the *geisha* here require similar assistance?

In the end, the veracity of an *obi* will hardly matter to AS7 because he'll have come to answer a far more basic question—one reserved for men of wealth and status. And the question is this: *do they or don't they?*

Kyoto

My imagination of Kyoto is reinforced with the *true fact* that I've actually been there. I've been to Gion, and have seen a geisha, or perhaps a *maiko*. A *maiko*, I guess. I was walking a narrow street lined with shops and houses in the traditional style, and the *maiko* posed for a photo at the entrance to one such building. She held aside one half of a *noren*—a kind of curtain that covers the top part of a doorway—and peered out from the opening.

"That's cute," said her friend taking the photo, a completely *normal-looking* young woman.

They continued what sounded to me like a mundane conversation, and I thought they made a very strange pair. But that's not all I remember of Kyoto.

In Kyoto I drank *sake* at a small restaurant with furniture made from bare two-by-fours (I've forgotten the metric measurements), stayed overnight in a capsule hotel, and caught up on my EcoRights work at a place called Popeye Internet Café. There I had a private booth with a computer and headphones, and a pair of tartan house slippers, which I didn't use. There were free soft drinks, and shelves of soft porn magazines and *manga* to borrow. It was good to have some space to myself, to get things done. But the smoke made me sick, made me think I should have been spending more time with Yoshiko and Stevie.

We were in Japan so Stevie could meet his extended family, and I think Yoshiko was trying to endear me to her country, as a place for us to live. To be sure, Japan had advantages for us—not least of which, Yoshiko could find work in her own language.

Things are getting weird here, she'd say, meaning here in North America. I told her things were getting weird everywhere, pointed out how much money I was making—told her I could depend on it for another five years or so, anyway. Pointed out how hard it was just *to move everything*. We'll move someday, anyway, I said. We don't have to rush.

Perhaps we should have gone sooner—but it's always so hard to know, at any one moment, *exactly what to do*.

secret rendezvous

As part of *Edo: Pleasure District in the 21st Century*, a container is now the site of an art installation. Through a peephole, one can see an actress, nude, lying on her back on an examination table, feet toward the audience. She is wearing a strap-on dildo with a three-strap harness (around the waist and thighs). The dildo is red and sharply pointed, and looks nothing like a penis at all. A number of wires attached to its base extend to a man on a neighbouring table. He is also nude and lying in the same orientation. The wires from the dildo attach with medical electrodes to four points on the man's abdomen. A third performer, a woman, is dressed in an anachronous nurse's uniform including a dress, apron, and cap. She repeatedly brings sheets of paper from a desk at the back of the container, and stabs them onto the dildo as if it were a bill spike. Each time she does so, the man twitches so violently that he lifts off the table, his body landing back on it with a loud noise. I admire his stamina and athleticism. The robotic concentration of the nurse is impressive, too. All the performers are painted entirely white, and for this reason I think they must be working within the *Butoh* genre. But no explanation is given for the performance—apart from the title Secret Rendezvous on a small white card above the peephole.

past life regression

The woman appears almost nightly—the one who says, "We're going to be together for a long time, eh?" I never have the presence of mind to take a close look at her. Or if I do, I can grasp only a single detail—perhaps her hair, the density of her arms, her skin tone, or her voice—but never, it seems, her eyes. I encounter her at different stages of life, and usually we are doing a domestic task together. She is slight, perhaps—or at least shorter than me. Sometimes I wonder if she is a stand-in for Yoshiko. But I think not.

Yoshiko is in my dreams, too—though not as often. In one such dream I'm driving a car with her in the passenger seat, and little Stevie is in his infant seat. There's a reptile in the car. The reptile is black—or it seems so because it is low on the dark floor. I feel it slither underneath, and I stomp on it violently. I stomp randomly in a panic, anywhere I can in order to kill the thing—and it seems I have killed it because it is nowhere to be seen. Or perhaps it is hiding. Or perhaps it has left the car. Where is it? I start to make suffocated, guttural sounds from the back of my mouth, as if parodying a *Noh* actor—an uneducated parody, by someone who knows nothing of *Noh*. Perhaps I am trying to scare the animal away, if it is still in the car.

And there are other dreams, too. Dreams without images, only sounds. For these I am partly conscious and try to wake myself. I want to verify whether the sounds are coming from the dream, or through the walls of my container. But my body won't respond, and I feel as if I am being pressed down. (I believe this is what the Japanese call *kanashibari*.)

The ocean container, and my dreams and thoughts inside it, rarely cause pleasure—and yet there is little enticement to go outside, apart from the temptations of *Edo*. I still don't want to encounter others, and doubt the change of scene would do me any good. It is a rare day when I feel there could be no harm in leaving, or that I am missing something on the outside. Rarer still are days on which I actively seek something there. So it is only the torment and confusion of my dreams that leads me, one day, to visit the woman in the VW van—the woman with the signboard for *healing practises*. The one like this:

HEALING PRACTISES (rates negotiable):
• yoga
• past life regression
• loving kindness meditation
• mother and infant acupuncture

I go to her door, and think to turn back. Do I really want to meet someone who practises *infant acupuncture*? But it's too late. She has seen me approaching, and comes out to meet me.

"So you're here," she says.

"Yes."

"Finally. I've seen you before."

"You have?"

(Immediately I am struck by this: she speaks lucidly, and shows no signs of cosmetic surgery. I am put at ease.)

"Are you—"

"I'm here for a consultation, actually. But I don't have much money, so—"

"It's by donation."

I show her some crumpled bills—the last I have.

"One of those will do if that's all you have for a while. Or you can get me next time. Regression? Meditation?"

"The former."

"I'm Alison, by the way. This is my daughter, Willow." She gestures to the young girl—the girl with Down syndrome. Willow takes her mother's hand. "Reed, my partner—you've probably seen him before. He's doing some work on the outside today. You don't have to tell me your name if you don't want to, but that's us."

"I've been having some dreams."

"I can maybe help you with that. But I want you to know I'm non-spiritual. In case it matters."

Non-spiritual. What does it mean? We go inside the van and I sit across from her on one of the facing bench seats at the narrow table beside a window with horizontally sliding panes. There is a lace curtain on the window, and the table is covered with a red gingham check cloth. Alison opens one of the kitchen cupboard doors and brings out a crystal ball on a wood base. She places it on the table casually—not with the reverence I would expect from a clairvoyant.

"It's to help me focus. And you, too."

I start telling her about my dreams, about the woman recurring in my dreams.

"We seem to share a domestic life," I say. "We fish, we collect salal berries together. We might even have a child—although I am not sure. It's hard to get a handle on things."

"So do you think it's about a past life? Or could it be the future?"

"I think it's—"

"Wait. There's another way to find out."

Alison unwraps a deck of tarot cards and asks me to choose one. By chance I take a card that, unlike the others, is merely a geometric design—infinity signs with a kind of iron cross built in.

"Fool," she says.

"How so?"

"Not you—the card. It's the fool, the origin. Without knowledge. The beginning of a cycle. The past. Choose another card."

The card I pull is blank.

"Is this my past?"

"No. It's the card that says, 'It's not for you to know.'"

Willow enters the van and sits next to her mother. Alison puts her arm around Willow, who puts her child hands on the crystal ball and looks into it. Alison raises her eyes and tells me to close mine. I oblige.

"I see a dark oceanic light. Wide rays of light from a distant surface of water. Inconsistent light refracted through the changing surface. Does it look familiar?"

"Are you asking *me*?"

"I'm asking you."

"Not really."

"But I hear a sound, too. A distant sound, calling for you. Like whale song. Does that sound familiar?"

"I've never thought of it that way, but—"

"Tell me what it sounds like."

I describe the sound. Low, like a diesel locomotive, and higher, too, maybe a trumpet, strangled and processed with reverb effects.

"It doesn't have to be a whale song, but it could be a sound from a past life," says Alison. "Or it might just be a memory from the womb. We never lose such memories. They are only obscured under subsequent layers of experience. If you think about your mind as a kind of archaeological site, if you keep scraping away the layers, going back through your memories.... What did you do yesterday, for example?"

"What did I *do* or what did I *think*? Or what did I *dream*? I don't think I ever really *do* anything."

"It doesn't have to be significant."

Alison tells me to keep my eyes closed, and asks me to choose another tarot card—by touch. There is silence but for the sound of a breeze and some occasional hammering from elsewhere in the compound. A nail hammered into wood, echoing between the containers.

"You are—and we all are—a vessel for what is constant. When I look into your past, I see a cycle of nature. It's still in you, but you rarely perceive it. Others sense it but they don't know what it is. You've been living in a world of lead and gold, but it hasn't always been a good match for you."

Lead and gold. I open my eyes and notice that Willow has left the van.

"So what should I do?" I ask.

"The blank card was space for the unknown. To know something is to limit it. Not knowing provides flexibility. You have to keep following the course of your dreams."

Alison opens the van's sliding side door and gestures for me to step outside. Immediately I hear a high squeal and see a large animal just outside the door, backing some steps away, startled. Alison tells me to stand still.

It's the tapir. I can see now it really is a tapir. It's glancing between us and Willow, who's been sitting on a three-legged stool feeding it. Willow has a carrot in her hand.

The girl says to the tapir, "Don't worry," and the animal slowly comes back.

"She's the only one," says Alison. "He won't get close to anyone else. Only Willow. He stays only because Willow is here."

manatees

Knowing the tapir is in the compound reassures me. I begin to think it might save us—might motivate those on the outside simply to let us be (to let me be).

I'm thinking now of a wooded area near my childhood home. It had a ravine with a creek running through it. Local ecologists noticed some rare plants in the area—not endangered plants, but plants unusual for the region: goldenback ferns, badge moss, ivy-leaved water-carpet, false bugbane, miner's lettuce.

Town council approved plans to develop the area: to harvest the trees, fill in the ravine, and build houses. In response, one of our high school teachers (a man who would later be slandered and driven from town) got some of us connected with the ecologists to raise awareness of the issue.

Ultimately we failed to save the wood, and I thought hard about why. My conclusion? The plants there were too boring for most people to care about. They were almost all uniformly green, and the birds there were all brown and not particularly shapely. The same can be said for the rodents.

What would it have taken for people to want to save those woods? Perhaps if there had been a manatee in the creek. Or a unicorn. Or a mountain tapir.

a butoh workshop

Edo: Pleasure District in the 21st Century is back, and I see that Edo has been quite loosely interpreted: today's workshop is on *Butoh*. The instructor—the *sensei*—is an older woman, perhaps in her late 70s. She speaks with a heavy Japanese accent, and tells us the names of the masters under which she studied in Tokyo. The names mean nothing to me.

"We wanted to focus on finding our *Butoh* soul," she says. "It doesn't matter where. Even we need to make money, we danced in strip club. We call it art stripping. But as long as our motivation is pure, we did it. That's how we keep the company alive. We were homeless, too, sometimes."

There is a long pause, and she seems to be looking at a spot somewhere in the middle of the blue plastic tarp on which her students sit. There are five of us. Predictably, Alison is here, too, but she hasn't acknowledged me. Her focus is on the *sensei*. Alison looks as if she is meditating, a kind of staged meditation, as if she wants to transmit her seriousness to all around.

"Anyway. Take off your shoes," says the old master. "You might have seen *Butoh*. A dancer almost nude, painted white, with just the *fundoshi* cloth. To some it is just spectacle, and maybe they are right. But to the dancer, it has to be about *Butoh* body—finding your *Butoh* body. It is cold today. I don't want to make you have to do art stripping today—no, no. But you have to take off your shoes. You have to have your naked feet, and now feel the plastic sheet on the soles of your feet. Soften your gaze...."

Thus begins a kind of walking meditation, during which we are reminded many times to maintain our soft gaze, to keep our distance from one another as we travel, and not to walk into any of the containers or tents. We are told not to act out any gestures, but to become them. The *sensei* tells us:

Feel the wood chips under your feet. Feel the mud. Place your foot in it softly. Ground is cold, but you know it is colder without the warmth you feel coming from the core of the earth. It's coming up through wood chips. Feel the minerals and rotting organic matter like connective tissue between yourself and earth. Like tendon between bone and muscle. You are the muscle. The earth is bone. With each step your feet hardly leave the ground. You are tilting on the earth, but really earth is tilting on you. You are hanging upside down from it. Your body is weightless. There is no pressure on your body. Now the sky is underneath you. You bring sky energy into a hole on top of your head. It is the bottom of your head now because you are hanging upside down from earth, and you keep walking slowly under the earth you turn upside down. Keep pulling in the sky. Keep walking forward until you find the ocean. You are on the ocean but just on the surface. Your feet rise up and down with waves. You can't penetrate the ocean, but the sky energy keeps coming on top of your head, filling the ocean. The waves are the breath of the ocean, breathing in and breathing out. You are feeding it with sky. You can see sky reflected on the ocean. Sky goes through you into the ocean. You see shapes of clouds on the ocean, underneath the ocean. Whale under the ocean. A fish. They are looking down at you walking upside down on the surface of the ocean. You are walking in a cloud of fireflies and you grab at them with your hands, pulling energy into you. Take them in through your mouth. Suck them in through the hole on your head. Keep bringing more energy into the ocean. And now you are riding on a very large wave, watching the contents of the ocean fly past on the other side of its surface. And you realize you are not wearing any pants. How do you feel? You can be embarrassed, or maybe you are proud. You are proud and maybe you show the fish.... [Etc.]

During the entire exercise we encounter no one from outside our group, and the compound seems to be deserted. Do we pass near the entry gate? Do the police or the volunteer Community Safety Patrol see us? I am not sure because I'm focused on the sky, the sky coming in through my head, the energy coming into the ocean—and all that, which is fine. But I want the *sensei* to bring us *inside* the ocean: for the most part we observe only its *surface*.

fragments of conversation

In addition to shipping containers there are many tents in the compound. And because the tents are thin and close together, many of their occupants go to the container alleys for private conversations. Most of these conversations are held in transit, as the participants walk by. So I hear only fragments:

A: Too much water can kill you.
B: Not enough water can kill you.

And:

C: Finally, I'm pregnant.
D: Are you going to have an abortion?

the prenatal class

Normally I wouldn't go to a fortune-teller, but a fortune-teller once told me I would have only one child, or an aborted child. Yoshiko and I hadn't known each other very long when she got pregnant, and we talked about an abortion, though not seriously. We knew we could have only one child, and perhaps that's why Stevie was born. It wasn't a hard decision, really, and we soon registered for a prenatal class.

The lessons took place over a number of weeks, during which I kept a record of my observations. My notes ended up being of little practical use, though they do make a story, which—like most stories—is a compressed retelling of highlights. We learned, for example, that orgasm flushes out the uterus after birth, and that it is fine to eat the placenta. And the instructor advised us to feed our newborn sugar water, but not to tell our doctors: "They'll say it's the wrong thing to do, but I assure you it is right."

He also showed us a film of primitive, pre-linguistic humans shot in realtime, for four hours, with no superimposed sound or cuts. In the final sequence they enter a forest and discover a portable stereo playing drone music. They crowd around the stereo and—without anything having foreshadowed this—say "hello" in several modern languages, as if expecting it to recognize one of these languages and respond. The film over, the instructor invited us to share our thoughts on what it had to do with childbirth—unless we thought it was "just too obvious."

We also visited a beach. It was a warm, early summer day, and some of us had planned an after-class picnic at a seaside park. There, one of our fellow students began to remove her clothes. She was a lithe and hairless woman, and did not look at all pregnant. She started doing cartwheels in the nude, then sat down and asked us to paint her entirely silver-grey, using paint and sponges she produced from a valise. After the picnic, she told us, she was off to the World Naked Bike Ride, and then to her part-time job: posing for tourists as a living statue. "The paint's metallic, but don't worry," she said. "It won't harm the baby."

So as not to betray any prurient interest, I started taking wide-angle "group" photos of our classmates and the cartwheeler. But just as the woman was having the insides of her thighs painted, Yoshiko grabbed the camera, walked right up to her, and took a close-up of the woman's vulva. "I believe this is the photo you wanted," she said, handing back the camera, the image aimed toward me on the view screen.

From time to time I have returned to the image—to the photo, that is—and have noticed it reminds me not of the event, but of a painting at the local maritime museum. It is an ornately framed picture of a small boat—perhaps a tugboat—ascending the slope of a menacingly large wave. Strands of sea-foam can be seen on the wave, which is stage-lit before a darkened sky. The cartwheeler's vulva is an uncanny scale model of this overpowering wave. And that's not all.

Something else I recorded in my notes is the description of a postcard I found on a table in the anteroom to the office in which the prenatal lessons took place. The image of a chair—like an Adirondack chair under a canopy of billowing fabric—facing the horizon on a tropical beach at midday. Beside the chair is a pistol. Now I often imagine myself in such a chair, sitting alone, with a bottle of wine.

possibilities

There are many possibilities. Things exist simultaneously that are different but equal. I am applying Clotrimazole to the fungus growing between my toes. Sweet Soul is shooting another music video in which she *actually does it*. AS7 is having a fancy lunch somewhere. Someone is dying alone in a hospital. A prisoner is defecating and notices the toilet paper no longer protrudes from the slot in her prison cell wall. (She thinks: Why can't they just give me a roll of toilet paper? Do they think I'll hang myself with it?)

And what else is happening? Someone is being crushed to death under the blade of a Caterpillar D9. Police shoot another prisoner in the back of the head—in *self-defence*. A family's apartment is targeted in an air strike and they burn to death. Such things aren't often at the forefront of our consciousness, but they happen.

false lily of the valley

As I wait for imminent release I've been following the path of my dreams—of forests, strange women, immersion in water, and yearning. I've never been partial to *yearning*—especially not books about yearning—so I must do something about it. The stuff of my dreams makes no sense to me, and I'm not satisfied just *to embrace the unknown*, or whatever Alison says to do. So I go back and tell her.

"You don't have to follow the cards' advice," she says. "It's your choice."

"I think I need to try something else. If you have any suggestions. Or a new reading."

"Maybe you need to do a purge. Maybe something more connected to where you are. False lily of the valley: I dried the young leaves and ground them up last spring. I don't know if it's the right thing to do with them—to dry them, to do a purge with them at this time of year—I haven't met any natives who can tell me for sure. I read somewhere it's supposed to be a spring purge, and I think it was part of a spirit-feast. You can try it if you like."

"Do I know it?"

"You've probably seen it in the woods. It's the low one with the waxy, heart-shaped leaves. Green berries with brown speckles."

"It looks like poison."

"It's not. If you wait a month or so you can pick some yourself around here—if you have a pass."

I say nothing.

"You can try the powder, or you can wait for us to bring some back fresh, when it's in season. We come and go a lot, to make a bit of money on the outside. But I do have to charge you for the powder, by the way. It was a bit of work to dry it and grind it up. If you want it." She names the price.

"I've got that much, anyway."

"But take it when you think it feels right. And if you need more, let me know."

She goes deep into the van and brings back a tiny zip-seal bag, half-filled with a dark green, almost black powder.

a white peafowl

If anything can be said, the VW Van Family (as I sometimes call them) seems to attract—and seek out—the world of nature. I notice now that a white peafowl has entered the compound, and I've seen little Willow feeding it birdseed.

The bird is male—it is the well-known Asiatic peacock, but white. It is not an albino because it has some minute colouring. It must have been bred this way, I think—I have heard of such animals being bred in captivity. I'm not sure how it got here, but I overheard someone say it was illegally imported, confiscated, and left here because no one knew what to do with it. I've seen it take short flights and fan out its white tail. There doesn't seem to be a peahen anywhere around, but I'm not outside enough to say for sure.

Whenever I've noticed the peacock, it's been running away from someone, but it doesn't run away from Willow. I've seen it eating right out of her hand.

"You are safe," she says.

container security

"I think you know I know a lot." It's 743, who's shown up unannounced at my container. "I'm taking the file from this point."

"It's what I expected."

"I think you need some reassurance, so I'll show you the plan."

He unrolls a sheet of A4-size graph paper, upon which is an inaccurate pencil-drawn map of the Pacific Ocean, framed by the northern coastlines of Asia and North America. Between the two sides is an unsteady line from the west coast of Canada to Japan, with an arrow point ending somewhere near Tokyo.

"This is how," he says.

"You must be joking."

"Yes. But you can post it on the wall above your bed."

I take the map in my hands and survey it for a long moment, to look for a detail that might have been missed.

"I just want to say," he continues, "that we're working on it. Every day I'm thinking of a way we can load you on something and make it so you can't be seen."

a poem

I write a few poems to pass the time. At this point they all need a few more drafts, to be sure, so I'm not quite ready to share them here. What I can tell you, though, is that one contains a reference to Courbet's *L'Origine du monde*. When I wrote it I didn't want to be too graphic, so I mentioned only the title. But why did I mention it at all? Because she showed herself. The recurring woman opened her legs to me and she didn't have any teeth there. In my dreams often there are teeth there. She was unafraid for me to see her, and *unafraid to be obscene*. And why would she? It feels as if we really do know each other—and I am going crazy to know where and when. But there is never a chance to ask. When I awake, I always want to go back and look around, but can't will it to happen.

And there was another kind of dream, too, incidentally. Someone handed me a chain-saw and told me to go hunting with it. But I don't recall what else happened. Like the dream with the woman, it was fleeting. In any event, I think it would be extremely difficult to hunt with a chain-saw. The target animal would need to remain very still. No animal would do that.

matsuri

Now, by way of *Edo: Pleasure District in the 21st Century*, we are having a *matsuri* in the compound. A real, simulated Japanese *matsuri*-style festival with a variety of *yatai*, or sales stands. One is selling *takoyaki* (octopus parts in batter), another is selling *yakisoba* (fried noodles). There is a tent at which one can enjoy *kingyo-sukui* (goldfish scooping). The "Secret Rendezvous" *Butoh* dancers have painted themselves gold and walk mindfully through the compound shaking tambourines and playing *shakuhachi*, bamboo flutes.

This real, simulated Japanese *matsuri* is very much like *a real Japanese matsuri* except that it is much smaller. The *yatai* area, for example, is but five meagre stands in a container alley. It is the length of just two containers—which is not to say I don't find it interesting.

At one of the *yatai*, a plaintive woman in a synthetic down jacket sits behind a table displaying trays of spare toy parts. She nods to me as I pass, not as if expecting a sale, but I think in solidarity. At another *yatai* someone sells various kinds of *anpan* (bread filled with red bean paste), all shaped suspiciously like penises and vulvae.

I remember a conversation with my Japanese father-in-law. I asked him once about *matsuri* merchants. He said: "They're all *yakuza*, you know."

underground

Alison takes me to a spot at the far end of the compound, which backs onto a forest. There are more containers than the compound can use, and here some empty ones are stacked two high. Because these containers are surplus rather than residential, the openings don't all face the same direction, and it seems easy to walk between them or even to get inside them undetected.

"Don't tell anyone about this," she says.

We enter an unlocked container and Alison asks me to help her lift a large sheet of plywood with some holes drilled in it off the floor. Underneath there's a circular opening. A ladder descends into the earth. Alison shines a flashlight down the tunnel.

"This took a long time to make. Someone had a stick welder. We had to take turns keeping watch."

"What about all the dirt?"

"Who knows. Some of it went to the community garden plot, I guess, but the cops couldn't put two and two together. You should try growing something there. It might do you some good."

"Is it an escape route?"

"No. Although it could be, I suppose. Mainly we wanted to see what was under here. To excavate the past. You know those old bottles in our van? This is where I found them. I don't know why we found so many bottles. And some other stuff. Anyway, if you can't go through or over the fences, now you can always go down, and that's something."

"Are you still working on it?"

"We stopped a while ago. I just thought you might want to see what happens if you go under here. You might find out what all those noises are, what those dreams are—if you get out of the compound a bit. Which you can do here, in a way. If you really concentrate you might uncover something. It's where I go when I really want to get focused."

"What about air?"

"There's plenty. The plywood doesn't flatten down completely, and there are the holes. There's a central shaft—it's pretty cavernous. Just don't go all the way down. We made it deeper than we needed to—like a reservoir. About three or four metres down you'll see a tunnel off to the side and some alcoves. Put the cover down when you go in."

Alison leaves, closing the container door behind her. I've got a mechanically charged flashlight with a wrist strap. I start down the wood ladder. It's awkward getting the cover back over the opening, and I have to brace myself against the tunnel wall.

The sides of the tunnel are surprisingly smooth. It doesn't take long before I get to the horizontal offshoot. Its roof is a parabolic arch, and every few metres there are simple A-shaped trestles, reinforced with crossbeams near their tops. The tunnel's tall enough only to crawl through, and the trestles make it difficult. I have to stop each time I want to see ahead. It's hard to crawl on all fours and keep the flashlight pointing forward at the same time.

When I stop to look around, I can't see where the tunnel ends (it curves to the left), but I do notice some openings coming up, leading off to the right—these must be the alcoves Alison mentioned. I keep moving forward by touch, without being able to see much.

It's silent here—there's really no noise at all, aside from my breathing and scraping along the floor. But I question whether silence will help me find what I'm looking for. And I wonder about the strength of the passageway. What if it collapses while I'm down here? What if I can't get the cover back open?

"Have you ever noticed that everyone here is some kind of archetype?"

The voice is close, right next to me. It comes without warning. Before this I'd heard no breathing or movement aside from my own. I hadn't imagined anyone else would be down here.

"Doesn't it bore you?"

I aim the flashlight in the direction of the voice. It's the shirtless woman with the electrical tape Xs and the leather jacket:

```
        I
        L
M K U L T R A
        U
        M
        I
        N
        A
        T
        I
```

"Like the girl," she says, squinting, putting a hand in front of her eyes. I turn my flashlight toward the ceiling. "The girl's, like, the *challenged gifted child* archetype. And her mother's, like, the *gypsy*—not that I've really talked to her. And I'm somethin', too. Even though I'm tryin' hard to be so original. And you're—who are you? I don't know what you are. You want some?"

She's sitting on her haunches and she passes me a hash pipe between the ripped knees of her jeans.

"What is it?"

"Kinnikinnick. I found it up on the mountains last summer. It's good. It makes you mellow."

"I think I'm okay. I'm not much into smoking things."

"What brings you here today?" she asks.

"Well—"

"I've seen you around, but you don't get out much, do you? Anyway." She waves her hand down the tunnel, as if she's suddenly no longer interested in talking. "If you want to get spiritual or whatever, there's another alcove just down a little ways."

I prepare to continue my journey.

"See you around, stranger." She holds out her hand to shake mine, and I reciprocate. Hers is surprisingly small, and somewhat clammy.

underground 2

I find my spot and sit just like she does, on my haunches, knees up. I turn off the flashlight so it's completely dark. It's a lot warmer here than I thought it would be, but damp. After a few minutes I notice water dripping from the ceiling, very slowly. I'm thinking of my clothes now. They must be a mess with all that bracing against the main tunnel wall and crawling to where I am now. My jeans must be soiled at the seat, knees, and shins. The back of my anorak, too. That will dry fairly quickly if I rinse it, but the jeans will get mouldy—unless I can just shake out the dirt. Unlikely.

At least worrying about my clothes overrides my concerns about the strength of the tunnel, now that I've settled in. It's like flying on an airliner. I've always been more worried before the flight than when I was actually on it. The experience of air travel is so static—the noise, the seating position, and the quality of light are so constant—that I feel nothing can go wrong. Even though falling from thousands of metres in the air is guaranteed death—if the aircraft happens to fall. One is more likely to survive a tunnel collapse than an air catastrophe. I'm certain of it. But I'm not so interested in death right now.

Aside from the occasional water droplet, nothing is moving: the silence is uninterrupted, so I have time to consider the built environment. When I touch the walls they feel solid—so solid I find it hard to believe anyone in the compound could have created this space. You'd have to know what you were doing. You'd have to be an engineer or something. Perhaps this tunnel was here before the compound, and they simply uncovered it. If so, what was it for?

In any event, I have to get down to business, to let the tunnel be: at this moment its construction is hardly my concern. Now that I'm here I've got to concentrate, to quiet my mind, to breathe slowly, to calm myself. I've got to return to an image of the woman. The one in my dreams. Perhaps I can find her where we left off, ask her some questions. First of all, who are you? And what are those low rumbling sounds? What are those reverb-soaked squeaks and whistles? Perhaps I'll hear them again, here in the tunnel.

But there is nothing. No matter how much I try to concentrate, nothing enters my mind. No story. No sounds. Just consciousness of the damp, and of daily concerns. What's my next meal going to be? I feel hungry. How long have I been here? More than an hour?

I have no choice but to give up.

On my way out, I notice the woman with the leather jacket has left without making a sound. But someone else appears—as soon as I open the cover.

"Did you *see* something?"

"No. Nothing."

"That's not what I mean. Did you see something?" It's 743. He motions toward the opening.

"See what?"

"Exactly. That's what I thought."

walking in a small space

When the short time I've been in the compound starts feeling like a long time, I find reassurance in noticing the outside world hasn't changed that much—therefore I can't really have been here that long. I'm basing this on my limited contact with the outside through newspapers and occasional conversations—overheard conversations. But can I say it hasn't been a long time if I start noticing changes in myself? To some extent I have noticed changes in myself, though I can't quite identify what they are.

In any event, if the outside world doesn't change, the changed me will certainly have a different relationship with it—when I am released. I can't stay here forever, can I? I'm thinking of Nazi concentration camp victims: even they, in the direst circumstances, knew the war would end in a few years and they'd be set free. Didn't they? Of course they knew it absolutely. So I can't see why I, too, would remain in this compound forever. It only makes sense to prepare for release.

In preparing for release, the most practical option, I think, is to use some of the skills I have obtained in the compound. When I survey these skills, my *Butoh* training, however brief, comes immediately to mind. To be sure, I will need many months or even years of training, and I plan to self-train. My goal is to found an entirely new school of *Butoh* dance, one that further develops the art of walking.

I'm sure you have noticed that when we walk, our arms provide counterbalance: as one leg goes forward, so does the opposing arm. You may also have noticed that movement of the arms can be subtle, and we can walk with no movement in the arms at all—if, for example, we are holding something. The counterbalancing motion is necessary perhaps only at high speeds. Noticing this, I am inspired to innovate: I am teaching myself to walk counterintuitively, with my left arm moving forward at the same time as my left leg, and my right arm moving forward at the same time as my right leg.

With enough practise—I am practising every day—I will become so adept at this counterintuitive walk that it will look natural. Then, perhaps, I can fine-tune it by integrating neck motion—perhaps diagonally to the front right as my left limbs move forward, and diagonally to the front left as my right limbs move forward: I believe this would provide the correct counterbalance at high speed. I notice that some birds use their heads for counterbalance when walking— the white peafowl, for example. Such birds are for the most part domesticated or semi-feral and confined to a small space, as I am. Therefore I should do as they do, and use my neck as a counterbalance.

It won't take long before I have perfected my walk, and when I am free I can teach it. I will teach *counterintuitive walking* workshops. Other artists will be interested in this technique and will want to combine it with their own. Counterintuitive walking could be a very obvious motion accompaniment for someone who can sing in overtones, for example. Perhaps I would do well to start training myself for that, too. One or both of these skills—alone, or in combination—could interest students of dance. This is how I will define my role in the world. I will promise to define my role only this way, and not the other ways I have defined it until now.

Perhaps I will be overlooked in the war on eco-terror if I can change myself. Now I just need to find someone who can ask, discreetly: Can he please come back? He is out of the picture now. What harm would there be in it?

escalate ultra

Here's some copy from a full page ad I found in one of the papers:

Just because you're producing unnaturally high amounts of CO_2 doesn't mean you have to breathe it. The new Escalate Ultra comes with its own supply of air. That's the Cadillac Way. Adapting to our new climate, keeping our economy strong.

the emperor and the courtesan

Beyond my own thoughts, and beyond whatever reading material I find in the outhouses, there is inspiration in the compound itself. There might even be reason to think the compound is a *good* place to stay—at least while we have *Edo: Pleasure District in the 21st Century*. If anything, I find this series (or road show, or whatever you want to call it) entertaining. And I try to find practical use for it, as a kind of training—if not for my counterintuitive walk, then for something else.

Following from the previous *Noh* and *Butoh* workshops, I have an opportunity to view an after-hours performance of a so-called *Noh opera*, or perhaps a *kabuki*, called *The Emperor and the Courtesan*. I believe it was funded, in part, by The Japan Foundation through the Consulate General of Japan. Only France and Japan, incidentally, continue to maintain funding for cultural promotion overseas. In Japan's case the total annual budget is, at present, equivalent to the price of a mid-market motorcycle. I suppose the amount allotted to *The Emperor and the Courtesan* might have paid for a stack of flyers.

Anyway, although it was very entertaining, I can't say I understood the performance entirely, and that may be due to my disinterest in the form, or my ineptitude with the finer points of Japanese. The "opera" would be very hard for me to describe, except to create my own approximation of the libretto. It could very well be subtitled *The Ignorance of the Foreigner*, and here it is:

THE EMPEROR AND THE COURTESAN
A Noh Opera in Two Acts

Dramatis Personae

- Emperor
- Courtesan
- Chonkina Choir (four actors)
- Wood Block Player

Costumes and Staging

The Emperor and the Courtesan are mid-stage facing the audience, stage right and left, respectively. The Emperor stands, or is seated on a table-height stool, and wears a neutral-expression *Noh* mask, a high-sheen *kimono* predominantly red with black borders, and white *tabi* socks. The Courtesan begins the performance seated on the floor in *seiza* position. Her face is painted white and made up following the custom, and she wears an elaborate wig. The top garment of her multilayered *kimono* has a white and purple cloud pattern, her *obi* is green, and she wears *tabi* socks. The Chonkina Choir also wear neutral expression *Noh* masks, and layered but lightweight (in comparison with the Courtesan) *kimonos*. They do not appear onstage at the same time as the Emperor and the Courtesan, and this can be achieved by way of a two-sided turntable stage, curtain closings, or whatever you like. Really, any of the instructions here are mere suggestions. The Wood Block Player, incidentally, is to one side of the stage, or offstage, and wears black.

ACT I

Emperor:

LUM! GLIAU! GLO! HLOL! GUU! SKHEU! SLEOU! HLAKH! GLEU!
FLO! LO! HOL! BLEA! FULEA! KLA! DOL! DLOCH! HLAKH! FLUONG!
DLIRU! FOLEU! KOU! NYEU! MAA! HEA! FLEKH! LUU!

(Each word spoken by the Emperor, and the amount of time between
one and the next, should be of consistent length. Each word begins
at a low tone, from the back of the throat, and ends at a higher tone,
at the roof of the mouth, so to speak.)

Courtesan:

Hai!

(The Wood Block Player strikes one beat on the wood block, and the
Courtesan removes one item of clothing.)

Emperor:

HEA! FLEKH! LUU! LUM! GLIAU! GLO! HLOL! HLAKH! GLEU!
FLO! KLA! DOL! DLOCH! HLAKH! FLUONG! DLIRU! FOLEU! KOU!
NYEU! MAA! LO! HOL! BLEA! FULEA! GUU! SKHEU! SLEOU!

Courtesan:

Hai!

(The Wood Block Player strikes two beats on the wood block, and the Courtesan removes one item of clothing.)

Emperor:

FLEKH! LUU! GLIAU! HLAKH! GLEU! FLO! KLA! DOL! HLAKH! FLUONG! DLIRU! FOLEU! HEA! KOU! NYEU! MAA! LO! HOL! BLEA! FULEA! GUU! SKHEU! GLO! HLOL! LUM! DLOCH! SLEOU!

Courtesan:

Hai!

(The Wood Block Player strikes three beats on the wood block, the Courtesan removes one item of clothing, the Emperor and the Courtesan leave the stage, and the Chonkina Choir arrives.)

Chonkina Choir:

Chonkina, chonkina, hai! Chonkina, chonkina, hai! Chonkina, chonkina, hai! Chonkina, chonkina, hai! Chonkina, chonkina, hai! Chonkina, chonkina, hai! Chonkina, chonkina, hai! Chonkina,

chonkina, hai! Chonkina, chonkina, hai! Chonkina, chonkina, hai! ...

(Continuing the above chant, the Chonkina Choir perform a simple dance to a rhythm set by the Wood Block Player. When the Wood Block Player stops beating the wood block, the Chonkina Choir freeze into poses, and the last choir member to freeze removes one item of clothing.

The entire sequence repeats, as does the entire sequence from the beginning of Act I, until at least the Courtesan is nude.)

ACT II

Emperor:

BLEA. DLIRU. DLOCH. DOL. FLEKH. FLO. FLUONG. FOLEU. FULEA. GLEU. GLIAU. GLO. GUU. HEA. HLAKH. HLAKH. HLOL. HOL. KLA. KOU. LO. LUM. LUU. MAA. NYEU. SKHEU. SLEOU....

(As the Emperor repeats his incantation in a softer tone than he did previously, he brings a *kokeshi* doll between his legs. The Courtesan stands up and walks with mincing steps to the Emperor. She kneels before the *kokeshi* doll, which she licks violently until the Emperor's "fruit is ripe" and the *kokeshi* doll's head bursts off. Thus the Emperor and the Courtesan are married: the *kokeshi* doll is a bottle of carbonated *sake*, opened to celebrate the marriage of the Emperor and the Courtesan. The Emperor parades his spent *kokeshi* doll before the audience, walking into the audience on his *hanamichi* or "flower road.")

Finis.

Note that the *after-hours* nature of the performance meant that the *kokeshi* doll of the libretto was in fact that part of the actor *in puris naturalibus*. There was more, but I left soon after the Wood Block Player made a gesture toward audience involvement, suggesting we all "match the bird to the nest."

rough justice

On the same night as *The Emperor and the Courtesan* I'm kept awake by Reed. He seems to be outside the VW van playing his acoustic guitar and singing at the top of his voice. Apparently he's drunk. He's sharing with all in the compound a rendition of The Chameleons' "Second Skin," and I must say he does a very good job. When he sings "I realize a miracle is due / I dedicate this melody to you," there is a humble fragility that might, under the right circumstances, bring tears to my eyes. And when he asks, "is this the stuff dreams are made of?" and answers, "no wonder I feel like I'm floating on air," he maintains the same quality with the higher notes, and I realize he has an excellent voice indeed. The man could have been a star.

It seems, however, that not all share my assessment. In the morning I find Reed sitting outside the van, on the bottom sill of the sliding door. There is a deep red bruise or scrape on his left cheekbone, and he has a bloody wad of tissue paper inserted into his nostril on the same side. Alison is pouring water over a wound on his forearm and preparing to dress it. Willow is sitting on his lap.

The same morning I find a guitar tuning peg just outside my door. It seems to have been left there intentionally. I return it to Reed and he thanks me. I don't know if it will be much help, though: I assume the guitar has been smashed beyond repair.

Outside my door I also find an inkjet-printed detail from Jan Brueghel the Elder and Peter Paul Rubens's *Allegory of Taste, Hearing, and Touch*. It depicts a peacock served in full plumage. I don't tell Reed about *that*.

If life is cruel, one best not examine it too closely.

victims of communism

There is a bulletin board in the compound. Sometimes it has notices for short-term jobs with negligible pay. Recently there was an official help-wanted notice from the Economy, requesting physical labour to put up a Monument to the Victims of Communism. All towns are to have one.

In addition to the paper notice there have been recruiters soliciting help throughout the compound. "Work available!" they call out, indicating where and when to assemble.

One morning there is a knock at my door and a young female voice announces: "There's work available this morning."

It's a voice I can't imagine ever laughing in a carefree way. I remain silent and hope she goes away, but she persists. "Hello? This is the last chance to get work on the monument. Anyone there?"

I remain still in my sleeping bag and hope she won't open my door. Thankfully she doesn't.

But five minutes later I hear another voice: "Won't you come and work with me on the monument?"

It is the voice of the man with two right eyes.

médicins sans frontières

"It's not easy keeping dry here."

"It's true," says 743. He picks up a copy of VCitibeat from the milk crate beside his sleeping bag. The paper is damp. "You can only do your best. Keep the door open a bit, and keep the heat on as much as you can."

"But I've got an infection, and—"

"The fungus?"

"That's right."

"Most people do, after a while."

"But my comrades are no longer coming around, and I'm wondering—"

"If we get any medical attention here."

"Exactly."

"MSF have been around a couple of times. Once they brought caseloads of this shit. Seems to work pretty well." He gets up from his camping chair, grabs three tubes of Clotrimazole from a cardboard box by the far wall of his container, and hands them to me. "Twice a day on the infected area. I really shouldn't do that, though."

"What?"

He motions to the box. "Leave it there on the floor. Apparently silverfish eat the glue. In cardboard boxes."

"It's more or less impossible to keep them away—in any event."

"True."

"Sleeping pills?"

"No."

"I suppose it wouldn't be an MSF thing, anyway. It's just that I haven't been sleeping much—not very deeply. Not that I'm big on drugs."

"Maybe just get out more. Try to get some air during the day. Or find a book on postmodernism. That usually knocks me out."

raven

In a state of partial sleep, I have another dream in which the woman appears. It takes place perhaps not long after we watched the boat burn down to the waterline. But she's not with me: in this dream I'm merely *thinking* about her, and have a feeling she's somewhere not so far away.

As I think about her, the word *slave* keeps repeating over and over in my thoughts. Or at least a sense of entrapment and wrong. I don't know if it refers to her, or to me. Slave. Surely it's not our will to be apart. I'm apart from everyone now, I think. Slave. Overwhelmed by the power of *everyone going thoughtlessly in the same direction*, but I'm not sure what that means: as in my previous dreams, the context is unclear.

The physical setting, however, is concrete: I'm on hard-packed sand. It's misty and grey but for a few scattered pieces of bleached driftwood. There is a steady roar of waves. These clues tell me I'm on a beach, though I can't verify this as fact. I can see only out of one eye, and not very far. It seems the other eye is swollen shut or damaged in some way. I am damaged elsewhere, too: one of my knees feels as if it's in the grip of a vice. I can't move, even though I try.

A bird arrives, lands on a piece of driftwood nearby. The driftwood is a log, really—a tree trunk. The bird is a raven, strikingly large. It stands on the tree for a long time. It looks around. Its head moves with jerky bird motion. It is so close I can make out the details of its feathers. I can see its milky, translucent interior eyelids: I see them slide back and forth across the surface of its eyes, like clouds across the surface of a planet seen from space.

Eventually the raven speaks to me, and I am surprised—but not *too surprised*. This is not the first time an animal has spoken to me. And since I'm not distracted by a feeling of surprise, I am able to focus on what the raven says:

I sure like to play.
Now I feel sorry for you:
you liked to play, too.

local history

The Book Van makes a return trip, this time promoting a theme. Perhaps the real purpose is to suppress lending of six-hundred-page fantasy novels with shiny foil-relief covers, which dominate the shelves. Of course I can't be absolutely certain this is what The Book Van people are attempting to do. However, I notice such novels have been reduced in number, and a section of history-related books highlighted. Fantasy novels are easy targets, I think. But what makes history—the featured theme—any more legitimate?

In any event, I find a book—a very reasonable two hundred pages—titled *Travelling the Historical Backroads*. It's a road-travel guide to the region in which the compound is located. It interests me because I likely won't be able to take any side trips during my internment, and also because I enjoy reading such books. Yoshiko and I often used them to guide our vacations with Stevie. My personal interest was in ghost towns—gold rush towns, in particular. This country has always been in the midst of a gold rush, to be sure. So what I really mean is *the late nineteenth-century gold rush*. I'm not as intrigued by what came after.

When I visit a ghost town I want to see wood-framed buildings that might have rotted and collapsed but haven't yet, or are in the process. I am attracted by the emptiness of ghost towns in which only a few such buildings remain. One needs to recreate by imagination what once would have surrounded them—the sense of touching through a curtain, feeling what once was real. It is the definition of real.

As for *Travelling the Historical Backroads*, I have never visited any of the towns listed, but I'm quite certain the book leaves out major details. There's one town called Wymar, and another called Takayama, but it doesn't say how they got these names. And it misses all the things that make these places purposeful today: the solitary Lithuanian who lives in the sagging three-storey frontier building called The Empire Hotel, the two-space public campground across the street, currently occupied by a young couple, drunk and in a state of high sexual arousal, a group of teenagers playing an ominous game in the woods by an abandoned railway line, the rusting bus with a stovepipe sticking out one of its windows, parked on a vacant lot overgrown with blackberry bushes. The book misses all these things, and it annoys me with its tales of *colourful characters* who initially populated such places.

To be sure, *Travelling the Historical Backroads* almost convinces me that a self-sufficient settler life was meaningful, and that life before the time in which I live was better in general. This is due not, perhaps, to the effectiveness of any argument put forward in the book, but to the highly ephemeral nature of my physical living arrangements. My container, for example, likely won't stay in this or any one location, and it won't be left somewhere to rot. And even if it were left somewhere to rot, it wouldn't evoke anyone's historical imagination, because it is in no way exceptional. No one will talk about any of the characters, *colourful* or not, who lived in shipping containers. On the other hand, perhaps it's better that way, or at least more *realistic*—if we apply the principle universally, to everyone: all should be forgotten equally. And why? Because, beyond simplistic narratives, everyone in conventional history has been an asshole, really.

Janet in the news

While visiting one of the toilets I find the following headline in the back pages of the national news section of *The Globe and Mail*: "EcoRights charts new course." I learn my erstwhile employer has "acclaimed Janet Bowker as Director, marking a decisive shift for the organization." The article quotes heavily from a press release, and I learn that at its recent national convention "EcoRights announced a 'new direction,' denouncing so-called direct action tactics as 'a thing of the past.'" I learn also that "next year the organization plans to roll out a 'CoolGreen' campaign, including an app to help consumers find 'all the cool stuff you can buy to green the planet.'"

Javelin

At a conference—I think it was called "Working for the Future" or something like that—I happened to have lunch with a guy who told me about owning a 1974 AMC Javelin (colour: fawn beige). He said that when you really put the pedal down, you could *actually see* the needle move on the fuel gauge.

view from a coastal mountain

I can't really judge someone who drives an AMC Javelin, or a stretched Audi S7, or any other decadent car. I've used up plenty of Earth's resources in my own way. Our family vacations, even if they were in a hybrid electric, required us to consume a certain volume of oil-derived stuff. I suppose everyone has a *right* to visit far-off places in the comfort of their own car—but what if everyone actually *did*? I recall, in my youth, writing a story in which an oil baron—the story's villain—takes luxury helicopter tours to survey all the places that will disappear as a result of his industry. He brags about being the last to see them.

Anyway, I've been thinking about some of the nicer places I've been, and one memory stands out: a family vacation with Yoshiko and Stevie to a small town on the west coast of Vancouver Island. There were sandstone shores with stunted pines turned permanently inland by the wind—like *bonsai*. And just outside the town was a rustic lodge with a few yurts and cabins at the top of a tall hill—at the top of a *mountain*, really—at the end of a long dirt road not too hard for our little car, but challenging enough. When we arrived it was late in the day and the sun was going down. I believe we were listening to Brian Eno's *Taking Tiger Mountain (By Strategy)*—the final track, the title track. We listened to the album on all our summer vacations to the coast.

We stayed in a yurt, and it was called "Yurt of Infinite Horizons" or something like that. It didn't have a number. It was built on a raised platform, a deck with a view to a maritime horizon at the distant end of a forested inlet. The sides of the inlet were impressively tall. We were at the narrow end, and it felt somehow like looking out the top of a funnel turned on its side. The horizon was clear, but nearby we were under cloud cover. The low evening sun shone with the precision of a flashlight between the parallel layers of sky ceiling and water. All the distant conical trees—new growth—were illuminated asymmetrically, golden green, like tiny brushstrokes. Or like fur.

Right after we checked in I wanted only to unload the car and sit on the deck with my family—for us to sit together and watch the scene change in the fading light. But Yoshiko wanted to put Stevie to bed straight away, to maintain his bedtime routine. I told her we didn't always have to keep the same schedule, that sometimes it was important just to be still for a while. When that didn't persuade her, I told her I'd sit outside on my own—and I did. I was annoyed.

Did I have a cold beer with me that night? Was I smoking some kinnikinnick, as we liked to call it? I don't remember exactly, but my agitation soon subsided. The sun was already below the horizon by the time I sat down, but it was still light, the underside of the cloud layer clearly illuminated. It was a rolling, wave-like form of cloud—something called *undulatus asperatus*, I think. If I remember correctly, a bird flew a straight line, disappearing between the inverted wave-tops, appearing again, off and on. Or perhaps I simply thought at the time it would be novel to see a bird flying through *undulatus asperatus*, and because I had the thought, it has become part of my memory. I think the bird would have been a cormorant flying strangely high, like a self-propelled black arrow.

In any event, the underside of the cloud layer consumed my attention until it was too dark to view anymore. Then I looked to the horizon. It was hard, in the fading light, to see distinctly where that ceiling of cloud ended and the clear sky began. (Would it be sunny the next day?) There was simply a very faint grey-yellow glow in the distance, and I wondered how we locate the transition from cloud to pure air. Is there any such thing as pure air or pure cloud? Is there a hard dividing line between the two? Is there someplace in between?

One thing for certain was I wanted to be alone for a while. Maybe Yoshiko knew that. Maybe she knew it even better than I did, and that's why she put up no resistance when I told her I'd spend my own time on the balcony.

It's true there's a part of me that just wants to be alone sometimes. But not all of the time—and not now.

What wouldn't I do now, for some family routine?

second letter from Yoshiko

743 passes me a letter from Yoshiko, tells me he "can't" say where he got it. It opens in the standard Japanese way, commenting on the weather, letting me know "the snow falls almost daily here in Kyoto." I learn Yoshiko has put together a photo album to help keep my memory alive for little Stevie. The letter is short, though. It seems Yoshiko still hasn't received my reply to the first one she sent. She speculates it's because she was being too hard on me about my "volunteers and everything," and she apologizes. She lets me know she's not angry, asks me to please write. She assures me "all the plans I make are with you in mind, and I know we'll be together again one day."

For the record, I did write a reply to the first letter—I gave it to Dave just as soon as I could. I'm certain of that.

the Aztecs

When troubled, I often reassure myself by considering the scale of my problem in the universe, considering that my problem, or indeed my life, is no more significant than a grain of sand, or a bubble in a bubble bath. It's a memory of my childhood to which I often return, my evening bath. While lying down in the bath I would observe the various parts of my body—my knees, my penis, my belly—making islands among the soap bubbles. I would notice the bubbles appear and disappear, and I imagined them as a kind of universe seen from afar. Each bubble's ephemeral life, its split-second demise, was equivalent perhaps to millennia in its own small world. I didn't know what my *islands* had to do with it, but I certainly considered that my existence, and this planet, might be no more than a transient bubble of foam—when we look at *the big picture*, as they say.

At EcoRights we'd often need to counsel our more enthusiastic members when they got into trouble—when they acted as human shields, for example, chaining themselves to trees or standing in front of bulldozers. Inevitably they were removed by police, charged as terrorists, and held indefinitely while awaiting trial. To the media we'd say we'd rather take the legal route. Direct action happens only when all other options have been exhausted. If people's voices were heard this wouldn't have to happen, etc. Then we'd get our legal staff involved, and the whole *kabuki*-like legal process would play out—*kabuki* because it was the same every time.

It was not only like *kabuki*, but also like Aztec ritual sacrifice—in which our detainees were of two kinds. One endured their consequences stoically or with pride, so I started calling them the Tezcatlipoca, as in the sacrificial embodiments of the prodigious Aztec god—the ones who were treated like royalty, who practised dances and were paraded around the capital city for a year prior to the ceremony in which their hearts were ripped out and their bodies thrown down the steps of the Great Temple. These were the ones who pumped their fists as they passed the cameras, recited speeches to Mother Earth, refused to acknowledge the authority of the court. They knew what the consequences would be and didn't care.

The other detainees were dismayed and surprised by the outcome of putting their bodies in the way of so-called progress. When I made visits to the detention centres for moral support, they were the ones who asked all the questions. What will happen to me? What will happen to my family? How long will I be in jail? What are the chances of getting off? Will I lose my job? They were tormented by speculation, and practically wanted us to wipe their asses for them—although I didn't use those words in their presence. In their presence I said:

I know this is hard. You've done a noble thing. In some small way your actions will have an impact. Someone had to take a stand and it was you. We don't know what will happen to you now and I can only imagine how difficult this must be. If it makes you feel any better, please think of your problems in the context of the universe, which is infinite. The universe is awesome and unfathomable. Compared to it, your problems are small. So please think only about the universe. Or think about the Aztecs and their ritual sacrifices. Think about the captured warriors forced to dance before the Aztecs, force-marched to the apex of temple pyramids where their hearts were torn out and their bodies thrown back down the same staircase they ascended. The pain of knowing what would happen must have seemed unendurable to them. But what is it to us now? We don't even think about what happened to them, and there's not even a record of their names. Your sacrifice is just about the same. It is very small. Why give it such great importance? What purpose is there in worrying?

My approach didn't always assuage fears, but I was right. And I'm taking my own advice now because, if anything, I'm the latter kind of detainee. If I were the former I'd just walk out of here and see what happens. Instead I stay, even though I know the result will be the same no matter what: something unpleasant.

For respite from my fears, every day now I perform a loving kindness meditation for all living things. Within this meditation, the most potent image I have is of a gazelle, the weakest of its herd, about to be taken by a cheetah. I send loving kindness to the gazelle. I ask it not to be afraid, and hope that by some magic it feels no pain. This is but one life, and there are others. A moment of pain is but a grain of sand in the universe. A life extinguished in one place will reappear elsewhere. It must.

come out

Someone has driven a car into the compound. Sometimes this happens. It's a new Volkswagen Passat, black. The driver remains inside, alone. He's smoking a joint. He's listening to Steve Reich's "Come Out" very loudly on the stereo. The same phrase, looped over and over, shifting out of sync, a beaten man's testimony dissipating to incoherence. I can hear it clearly, even though the car's windows are closed. As interesting as they may be, however, this strange automobile and its occupant are among the more mundane discoveries I have made in the compound as of late.

Are you aware, for example, that tapirs have rather unusual feet? Tapirs are classified as odd-toed ungulates, which means they have an odd number of toes on their rear hooves—in this case, three. There's little to which I can compare them, so it's hard to describe these feet accurately. But perhaps they look like round paws with three elongated fingers, each of which is like a horse's hoof in miniature.

I have an opportunity, now, to examine one of these feet in detail. It has been amputated and left just outside my front door. Pinned to it is a small piece of paper, with a handwritten message:

From which eye does the first tear fall?

PART THREE

My gaze is that of a man meditating, lost in thought—I admit it. But yours? You cross archipelagos, tundras, mountain ranges. You would do as well never moving from here.

ITALO CALVINO, *INVISIBLE CITIES*

I have been told never to *expect* an earthquake.

My biggest fear has always been that an earthquake might happen at an *inconvenient time*: when it is dark and I have forgotten the location of a flashlight, in the early morning, when I don't want to leave my bed, after a meal, before I have had time to brush my teeth, when I am wearing no pants because I sleep wearing only a shirt, and am frozen between choices of just running outside, or first finding some clothes and then running outside (despite having read it is best to stay put during an earthquake). It could happen when I am lying on my bed, on top of the sheets, masturbating near a window or a large glass object that shatters, sending shards of glass flying through the air toward my genitals. Or it could happen before I get around to the precaution of putting shoes under my bed—leading again to cuts and bleeding, if I have to walk barefoot over broken glass. (The thing that scares me most about earthquakes is glass.)

Of course I know earthquakes are not scheduled events, so they *never* happen at convenient times. However, even though you may agree such is true in the so-called real world, you might object to an earthquake happening right now, here in this notebook. Perhaps you have noticed the pages that follow this passage are fewer than those that precede it. (In other words, this story is going to end soon.) So, in a tale such as this—one that seems to have no single aim leading naturally to *an explosive moment*—it may not seem to you *merely inconvenient* to have an earthquake at this point, but *transparently contrived*. I assure you, however, this earthquake is not an act of contrivance. Rather, it is a very real earthquake for a very *real* story. It could have happened at any point—even on the second page. Furthermore, an earthquake is not in itself a reason to stop telling a story or *to wind things down*. If this story is going to end soon, there are other reasons that have *nothing to do with an earthquake*.

the onset

The earthquake starts at about two o'clock in the afternoon, on a day in the middle of March. I am in my container, taking a nap on the inflatable mattress. The container begins to shake, to wiggle. It wiggles lightly at first like...like *fucking*, that's what. Then it starts going more vigorously and something is creaking—the hinges of the door perhaps. The shaking intensifies, this time like final thrusts before an orgasm—but it doesn't stop! And then it is not only wiggling, shaking, but also bouncing on the earth. Surely the container will slide away from here, I think. It is bouncing so hard I can't stay on my mattress! It is bouncing *very* hard, and I know it is because the Kroby lamp slides across the floor, hits the wall, and shatters. My container, now dark, is being dropped like a pile driver. That is the sound it makes.

my son

After the shaking is over, I think immediately of my son. Where is he now? What time is it in Japan? Will I see him again? I have survived—for now. But there might be aftershocks.

I remember a time just weeks before Stevie left with Yoshiko for Japan. It was around the time of his first birthday, and the two of us—he and I—were at a playground. And there, as I was pushing him on a toddler swing, he spoke to me in perfectly fluent Southern Tsimshian. Nothing presaged his use of the language, and until then I was unaware he spoke any language aside from his esoteric infant words. I don't speak Southern Tsimshian myself, so you may wonder how I knew he was speaking this extinct language. Simply, I *knew*. For just a minute or two his speech patterns changed and I knew not only that little Stevie was speaking a language, but also the name of the language, and the exact words spoken:

Now, papa, I can hear the sounds of the playground—the rattle of a chain bridge, the squeal of a seesaw, and the voices of children. This thing I'm riding creates a mild vertigo—like I feel in an elevator, where you let me push the buttons—and there is a mildly cool, late summer breeze on my face. In my field of vision, the horizon rises and falls. So does an ever-changing tower of cumulus cloud, in relief against the sky, in the afternoon light. I look into your eyes, and I know that you're a good person. And a pretty funny guy, too, sometimes. You like to make me laugh. I know you like being around me.

Of course I won't remember all of this exactly, but I will remember the feeling. And I will feel it even when I am a big boy. Even after you have gone.

at the lake

I think, too, of our last family camping trip—to our favourite lake. It's within driving range, one gas tank (return trip) from our family home. Just far enough to feel like an escape from the city, but not too far. I never tell acquaintances what the lake is called, because I don't want to see them there. I don't want crowds of people to invade this place. It's where I spend time alone, and with Yoshiko and Stevie.

I have one particularly strong memory of the lake from the year before last, in the autumn. Year after year, autumn—early autumn, at least—gets drier here, the difference between day and night temperatures more extreme. And so it was during the overnight stay of my memory. We could barely get warm in our tent, and breakfast was around a campfire. The afternoons, though, were hot like the top of summer—for just two or three hours. Two or three hours of bright sun at a lake high in the mountains, low angle sun making hard shadows of mountains on mountains. Bright sun directly in our eyes, so hot we could be comfortable without clothes—as I imagine it must be above the Arctic Circle on the longest day of the year. The dry breeze was like air from an electric hand dryer: although the water was almost ice cold, I was warm and dry within minutes of getting out. I could see, in the bright sun, beads of water evaporating from between the hairs of my arms and legs. And even the fine hairs on the backs of my arms were evident in the light.

I should add that the lake has a vast, sandy beach—a sand bar on a gradual incline receding from the waterline for perhaps ten metres or so before it drops off suddenly. Here the mountainside is broken, briefly, by what I suppose is silt from the nearby stream. How long did it take to build up like that? I'm not qualified to say.

The water at this lake is always clear, and in my memory there are kokanee salmon in the shallows. Tiny kokanee salmon. I understand they never grow beyond 35 cm, and these are but a fraction of that. Kokanee is to my understanding the only landlocked species of salmon. They evolved—or so I am told—from populations of sockeye that once had direct routes to the Pacific, but no more. They exist in lakes all around the North Pacific—on both sides, from Oregon to northern Japan.

On the afternoon of my memory, I am swimming out and returning to shore, swimming out and returning to shore. Yoshiko and Stevie are on a blanket on the sandbar. I'm thinking of *the expedient distribution of my libido*—or something like that. Something Freud wrote. In any event, I'm thinking of my strange obligation to Yoshiko and Stevie. What is it? And I'm thinking of a woman's sublimation, a kind of resentment, perhaps—although Yoshiko never seems to show it. Or at least I never perceive it.

outside

My container has been slightly malformed by the torsion. It is hard to get the doors to open. They aren't visibly bent, but the tolerances are off just enough that they're pressed tightly against the frame. I have to pad my shoulder with my sleeping bag and take a run at the doors to get them open.

Outside it is silent—almost like a city-silence at night during heavy snowfall. Based on the level of shaking, I expected to see slopes crumbled off mountains, but no such thing has happened. The containers, however, have changed their locations: they are no longer in perfect rows. This seems to confirm it was indeed an earthquake that happened.

I notice others have come outside before me. As I walk down the now crooked alley, someone invites me up to the top of his container, where he stands with a number of our fellow inmates. I accept the invitation, raise myself on a couple of milk crates stacked beside the container, and get a hand up the rest of the way.

"Look," he says, and points out to the estuary, beyond the mouth of the fjord. In distant clouds, in the direction of the city, there are spheres of spectral light—two spheres. One maintains its intensity, and the other begins to fade. I believe these are called *earthquake lights*. Then there is a slight aftershock, and I decide to come down.

I continue my walk through the compound, hoping to find 743. As I enter the alley in which his container is located, I see a man lying face down on the bark mulch. I can't see his face, but I recognize the hairline and clothes. I notice, too, his body is twisted in an impossible way—a way I don't want to describe. It seems too cruel, to me, that a body should be contorted this way—especially if it gave no consent.

It is the man with two right eyes, clearly dead.

743, yet again

When I get to 743, he's in his container with the door open.

"It's a good thing I kept this packed up," he says, indicating a glass water pipe—a *bong*, to be precise. Off to the side is a small cardboard box, roughly torn open, with ripped pulp cushioning and foam peanuts scattered on the floor. "I've been saving it for an occasion like this."

I notice the Thich Quang Duc hot air balloon poster is still up on the wall—such things are made to survive earthquakes. His Kroby lamp, however, is nowhere to be seen. 743 starts breaking up some marijuana and stuffing it into the holder at the top of the pipe stem.

"If you've got some time, there's lots I've got to tell you," he says. "About your comrades over there. Why you're here. Why I'm here. What you can do to get out of here. About the VW guy. About the guy with two right eyes."

"He's dead."

"I know. And I've got something to say about that. And other news, too. The tunnel has collapsed. If you go back there you'll notice a few of the containers have fallen into it."

"That's terrible. I hope no one was down there when it happened. It really is a shame because—"

"Do you want some of this?"

"I haven't smoked in quite a while."

"It's pretty mild. You might as well. There's not a lot to do right now, anyway."

So he mostly talks, and I mostly listen—and smoke a bit, too. And I don't know how long it takes, but by the time he finishes telling me everything—and I should add it's the first fully concrete discussion we've had—it's dark outside.

"I'm going for a walk," I say.

"You can walk anywhere now. No more cops at the gate. I guess there's too much happening in the city. Guess they need all hands on deck. Must be a mess down there. Must have been the epicentre—not that I'm qualified to make that assessment."

a forest, an arrow

As 743 says, there's no one guarding the pass gate. I walk out of the compound, straight into the forest, not far from the chain-link fence. There seems to be a trail—or at least there's enough space between the trees to imagine one. I can see because there are clear patches of sky, the moon reflecting light into this space.

I don't know where I'm going, but on the trail—if it is a trail—I notice an animal walking beside me. It overtakes me, as if to guide me. Based on its size and shape it must be a wolverine. What is a wolverine? Something between a dog and a ferret? I've seen them only in pictures until now. I decide to follow the animal, and we go deeper into the forest. After a while I can't see where the edges might be. The ground gets softer the deeper we go. Soon the wolverine stops, and so do I.

"Here," he says, pointing his muzzle to a small, mossy clearing. Then he leaves.

I sit down, and I think this forest must be very green in the daytime. There are ferns all around, and moss on the ground and hanging from the trees. But it is still too dark to see things clearly, so I close my eyes and concentrate on tactile sensations—in particular, the cold dampness seeping from the ground into my pants. Then I run my hands along the moss and find something smooth, tooth-like, and sharp.

I hold it tight in my hand, and soon feel even more dampness, this time warm—the breath of another, very close. I'm gazing into the face of *that woman*. Who is she? I know I've been with her before, right here, doing this. She's lying over me. I have an erection and can feel her moistness on my glans. I'm about to enter her, but let go of the object. The image and feeling disappear.

I bring the object back into my grip. This time I am deep underwater. There is only faint light, and sound that seems to have travelled a great distance. Low, reverberating sound.

Next I see a lateen-rigged boat, wrecked on the shore, and a stranded man from far away. He talks to me but I don't understand what he's saying. Yet I feel as if I know him.

Then another figure, standing some distance from me, in the forest. Moon-like face, expressionless, eyes and mouth black holes for the world close by. Arms stretched forward. In each hand a clamshell filled with clear liquid. The figure raises its arms slightly, gesturing to me like a seller at a market. *This must be for you, surely.*

"No, no, no," I say. "Not yet." I shake away, as if from paralysed sleep—*kanashibari*. The woman is back.

She is older now. Strands of grey in her black hair. We stand at the edge of a clearing, and we talk—this time in a language I comprehend.

"How will you know?" she asks.

"This is how."

I flex my bow and shoot an arrow into the trees.

switching yard

I walk out of the forest. It seems an easy thing to do. I enter a railway switching yard—the one beside the safety compound. It's submerged in fog, so I can't see clearly, but I know it must be the right one. Where else could this be? Grey fog and steel rails in the darkness. Nearby, oily gravel rail beds, creosote-soaked railway ties, a discarded railway spike.

In my childhood there was a train derailment near my home, and I remember taking a railway spike as a souvenir. It was an exotic treasure, and I used it as a paperweight. But the one I find here—despite being the same kind—seems like a facsimile, hardly important. Why is that?

There's a pack of cigarettes in my pocket. I don't smoke, so I must have got it from 743. Inside the box is a lighter. I sit down on one of the rails and light up. It's completely silent, and after a few drags I notice the small, crackling sound of the tobacco burning. It's the scale model sound of a much larger fire. I need to hold the cigarette some distance from my face—unfortunately I didn't bring my reading glasses—to observe the orange glow pulsing and winding through the burning end. I see it as a small city viewed from very far away at night, as from an airplane. Perhaps that's what it is. If so, it must be a very hot city. Too hot for humans to survive, if scaled to proportion.

Having given some thought to my cigarette, I notice now that a train is upon me. How did it arrive so unexpectedly? The locomotive's three headlights are surprisingly bright. Its engine rumbles loudly. Should I run? Where is this train, exactly? All these rails seem to crisscross one another, and I'm not sure from which direction the train will arrive. I can't tell even if I'm between two different tracks, or two different *rails*. If I knew I was between two different tracks I would feel safer. There's no telling where I am, so it's probably best to stay put, I think.

The train passes, perhaps two lines behind me. Very close, but far enough. I sit and feel the ground rumble. I concentrate on the sound of the wheels, clicking across the segmented rails.

At the same time, I consider a small city at the end of a cigarette.

reach for the stars

The sound of the train is distant now. It is so faint I question whether the sound is real, or something I have continued in my imagination. It must be safe, now, *to move from my position*. But I am not sure *where* it is safe—or even possible—to go from here. Because it may not be safe to go anywhere, I decide to return to the compound.

It is dawn, or even pre-dawn. I can see more than I did before—or at least I imagine so. I notice, too, it is the verge of spring. The air is damp and cold. It feels like something might start to grow in this air, which is why I have to go back to the compound: something is stirring and I want to find out what it is.

I have seen this rail yard from the compound many times before, so I know how to find my way back. I'm getting closer to the tear in the chain-link fence. Since the cops aren't there, I could also use the main entrance. But why would I?

The mist is dense but lifting. It holds back the progress of morning, but I can tell by the type of light that morning has already been established. The sun through the fog is at an elevation I might almost touch.

I see my original exit point just beyond the gravel of the rail yard, lined with damp grass. Approaching, I receive the distant, mid-frequency impression of a pop song on small speakers. Listening to identify this distant, fragmentary music, I reflect that—aside from *the same old crap*, a genre immune to influence—a distinctive feature of the music of this decade (or perhaps of this century) is that samples and fragments inform the melodies created on live instruments, rather than the other way around: things encountered by chance, or in part by chance, are now reproduced with intention. I make this reflection because, at a distance from the fence, all I can hear are fragments. Closer, however, it becomes easier to place what I hear within a genre—or perhaps within a category more precise. I recognize it as a song by D.A.F., about which Wikipedia (as I recall from memory) has this to say:

> Deutsch Amerikanische Freundschaft, or D.A.F., is an influential German electropunk/Neue Deutsche Welle band from Düsseldorf, formed in 1978.... In interviews they claim not to target anything or anyone specific while creating lyrics to be taken as a pastiche of language in the public media.... The album *Alles Ist Gut (Everything is Fine)* received the German Schallplattenpreis by the Deutsche Phono-Akademie, an association of the German recording industry.... The members of DAF, like other late twentieth-century popular musicians, have established an apprenticeship franchise [citation needed] with more youthful musicians, so that their music and/or style of music will continue after death—in much the same way as *kabuki* or *Noh* theatre troupes continue their art across generations.

The song is "Greif Nach Den Sternen" ("Reach for the Stars"), from the album *Gold Und Leibe*, released in 1981. When have I heard this song in the compound before? Never. So perhaps there has been a new arrival.

There is a slight breeze. The clearing mist drifts slowly through the compound, over the gravel and bark mulch and between the containers. The mist is like dry ice on the set of a war film—a film of the Great War. Is it dry ice they use? In any event, I now can see the source of the music.

In front of a light grey shipping container an old man sits on a yellow milk crate. He must be the owner of the music, broadcast from an orange plastic boom box, which looks as if it were designed for camping trips. He looks like an 80-year-old version of Mark E. Smith, and perhaps he *is* Mark E. Smith (although I would need to know when Mr. Smith was born in order to calculate his age at this time). He is an old man, and an old *rocker*. This is clear from the leather jacket and the jeans and the cigarette he is smoking and the discarded beer cans all around. And he is tired. He has had *a long night,* but he is watching a performance, being patient. He is watching a young woman dance. Perhaps she has had just as many beers—but for her the night is *still not long enough*. I identify her as the one with the design on the back of her own leather jacket:

```
              I
              L
    M K U L T R A
              U
              M
              I
              N
              A
              T
              I
```

She's the one with the Chelsea haircut who wears nothing beneath her open leather jacket but electrical tape Xs over her nipples. Normally she wears jeans and Doc Marten boots, but this morning she is wearing only the boots and lacy, *fundoshi*-like underpants so minimal she might as well wear nothing at all. These underpants barely conceal her vulva. She is dancing like Brigitte Bardot in *À coeur joie*, spasmodic and thrusting, to the ominous sound of D.A.F., heavy reverb crash cymbal and gurgling robotics. But—perhaps owing to the music—she is not smiling like Brigitte Bardot.

Another man walks through the scene quickly. He is middle-aged, balding, and dressed in denim. He carries a 2 x 4, and wears a leather tool belt with a nail pouch and hammer—as if on his way to a construction job, perhaps to repair something in the compound.

He says: "That's some sexy underwear you got there, Chelsea."

"Thanks," she replies, neither looking up, nor pausing from her agitations.

disappearing world tours

I return to my container, and decide to stay—this time for good. I decide with the immediateness of an earthquake. One moment I am free to come and go. Next, I remove the choice. I will stay inside. The change is sudden, but not without reason: my time in the compound has been a kind of regression, moving backward into myself—and I think I have found something there. I'm not sure yet what it is, but I must concentrate if I am to know. Toward this goal, going outside is a waste of time. I can't confirm that what I've experienced outside is any more real, or any less real, than what I've experienced inside this ocean container. So I stay.

Inside is real, and I think everyone understands that now. There's even a company called Disappearing World Tours. They bring tourists to the Rocky Mountains on a bus with no windows. The tourists never leave the bus. They watch nature videos. Videos of the Rocky Mountains. They watch the movie *Avatar*. Just like those tourists, I can remain in this container, and I *should*.

If you do not question *why*, perhaps you will question *how* I will manage to do so. You might question *how realistic* it is to stay inside. Foremost is the question of piss and shit. What will I do with them? To which I answer: it's not important. I won't be eating anymore.

As you can tell, this story is coming to an end.

And toward that end, the physical body is no longer important.

Except, of course, that one needs a body in order to control *a writing implement*. So I will hurry up and write a few more things.

endangered species

The world is disappearing and so are its species. Hundreds of species, perhaps a few thousand species, die off forever every year. In any event, it's happening far more quickly than the background rate of extinction.

Before a species disappears, it may have followed an evolutionary branch for perhaps tens of millions of years depending on where it began. And yet this is not long enough, in many cases, for humans to have taken notice. Many organisms go extinct without a trace, and we never know what they were. They are gone before we notice them.

At EcoRights I once suggested we pursue a campaign to raise awareness of this fact. Our slogan was to be, "For the species that don't exist." I thought a surprising slogan would be catchy. I thought it might provoke our audience to question further, to seek a point of reference. But I suppose most people don't really like surprises. My proposal was voted down. Someone said: "People don't believe in what's not real."

a new species of bear

Regarding all the many heretofore unknown, soon-to-disappear species, it seems my container is the correct environment in which to find them. To be sure, it goes against intuition to stay inside to find something new—assuming you believe discoveries can only be made outside. Yet I assure you this container is as good a place as any.

Recently I discovered a new species of bear, no larger than a fly. It was so small that at first I thought my vision was at fault—that perhaps it really was a fly, its bear-like shape only a visual distortion. But then I put on my reading glasses and confirmed that, yes—in fact it was a tiny little bear! It seemed strange a bear would be so small, but then I recalled that, as an adaptation to climate change, reductions in body mass have been observed in other species as well. In salamanders, for example.

Anyway, you may wonder if I was afraid to find a bear in my container—which of course I wasn't. How could I be afraid of a bear so small? If it were to slash me with its tiny little claws, I would hardly feel a thing! Keep in mind, too, that I noticed not just one, but five of these bears—and still had no reason to be afraid.

In addition to their small size, I have observed that these bears are not very fast—a clear deficit for carnivores feeding on other animals. Most animals of a comparable size are faster—woodlice being an exception. But even these create difficulty for the miniature bears. I think the bears would have more success if they organized themselves into a pack—but that is not the nature of bears.

Following from my observations, I fear this tiny species is not long for the world. It likely will go extinct within years, or even months or weeks. And even though it has taken perhaps a million years to arrive at this point, the tiny bear has been discovered only at the tail end of its existence, and will remain unknown to anyone but me. It will die, and will not leave any fossils. It will not be encased in amber. It will just rot.

AS7 in Ottawa

And what about me? Will I rot? I think not. I have hope because a man—the one I refer to as AS7—will soon file his report. He has just arrived in Ottawa, a nice city with parliament buildings and a variety of super luxury hotels, where the dining is fine, and the strippers—both male and female—have adjustable breasts and are able to do tricks with ping-pong balls. A paradise.

AS7 will file his report, which relays intentions from Japan and concludes with recommendations. There might even be papers ready to sign. If so, the Prime Minister will sign them because he is a reasonable man, amenable to good sense. He has his own opinions, to be sure. Of course they are not *my* opinions, but they are equally valid. All ideas are equal, even though they are different. They are *just ideas*. The Prime Minister will see this. He will empathize with me when he realizes I arrived at my ideas through a process similar to his own. He will see how simple it was: I turned one way, and he turned the other. I told people it was bad to keep blowing toxic gases into the atmosphere, and he told them it was good. And why not? What's any better or worse about that? After all, it was merely a coincidence we didn't arrive at *the same idea*, and the Prime Minister knows this. His idea has prevailed, of course—so it must be for the best. It was just *one idea* equal to all other ideas.

So I imagine the Prime Minister feels a kind of victor's benevolence, and that when we meet he will perhaps hold me in his arms and say: "I am sorry you suffered. I have won, but that is enough. All is forgiven. You are free to go."

Surely that is what he will say.

In return, I will kiss him on the lips. I will kiss him deeply. I might even put my tongue right into his mouth. And why? Why not! If there's one thing a Prime Minister requires—moreover, if there's one thing I really *should* provide—it is the appreciation of a subject.

a piano recital

I have forgotten to mention that, just prior to the earthquake, the compound was treated to a very lovely piano recital. It was titled "Fundraiser for the Victims" (although I am not sure *which* victims, or who among us could have afforded a donation), and it was put on by the Junior Academy Music School. They brought a grand piano to the compound, and set it up not far from my container. This meant I could see it clearly through my cracked-open door—except when my view was obstructed by the children's parents walking back and forth. The parents seemed to make up most of the audience. A number of the fathers were taking photos, and I overheard the following exchange:

> A: I picked up this lens just this morning. There was a power failure at the camera shop.
> B: Is that so.

At the recital, the first performer was a teenage girl, perhaps fifteen or sixteen. She played Beethoven's "Moonlight Sonata." Next, a slightly younger girl played "Maple Leaf Rag" by Scott Joplin. Then a boy, perhaps twelve, played "Chopsticks"—it seemed far too simple for him. Then another girl, and another boy, and I noticed the children were getting younger and younger. Eventually a newborn in a bassinet was placed on the piano stool. All of these children—even the newborn—were dressed in formal attire.

For the final performance, a foetus played a beautiful rendition of Chopin's "Minute Waltz" (Op. 64, No. 1). The foetus was still in her mother's uterus. The mother sat on the piano stool with a perfectly straight back, a hand resting on each thigh—her own hands, the mother's own hands. The foetus played telekinetically. I could see the piano keys move. I don't even have words....

Zoltar

Everywhere I look now, there is evidence the world is becoming kinder and more reasonable. On my final entrance into the ocean container, I bring a small stack of newspapers—just in case. Among them I find evidence of the kindness and reason to which I refer. I learn, for example, that even the US President has become a softer man, able to see himself with objective distance, willing to change his ways. He has denounced violence, and is undergoing hormone therapy. He says: "I am in transition to the next phase of my life." He says: "I want everyone to know the real me." The President will breastfeed victims of US aggression, because he is a man—now he is *someone*—who has compassion for others. That's because, in his own life, he has come to understand hardship: all his presidency he has been dogged by allegations of having been born in Ireland, because his name is O'Bama. But now he will remake himself as Zoltar, after the androgynous villain from the cartoon *G-Force*. Apparently the former Governor of Tokyo is "very pleased" by this display of affection for Japanese culture, and will soon visit the President in a hot air balloon shaped like a scrotum—to "showcase Japanese technology."

O'Bama is a man of peace.

something else

As further evidence the world is changing, I hear (I'm not sure where, but I know it's true) that somewhere another internet is under construction. On this fledgling internet, ideas are traded without third party permission. Alternative currencies circumvent transit hubs. I'm thinking about how this might affect the current regime, and I'm moving toward a possible answer. I think *something is about to change*.

Through the ocean container, I travel down a spiral tunnel to the bottom of something like a very deep boat or a floating city—something self-contained. I follow the tunnel without turning back, and come up next to the same point at which I entered. I think the path down might be the same as the path up: the tunnel's descending and ascending segments seem to be interlocked—like the shared yet divided home of fraternal twin gastropods. Perhaps anywhere along the route I can push through and cross over.

I take this image, and now I think...what I'm thinking now is *not* an interlocking path, or an interlocking world. This time I'm thinking of liquid—liquid filling a mould cavity. Not because it wants to mimic the shape of the mould cavity—a medium with its own currents and transmissions—but *to circumvent* these currents and transmissions. Like an insulating substance filling the spaces of an electrified metal mould cavity. Ceramic, perhaps, waiting patiently for the metal to rust away. In the meantime, it becomes something else that—while it cannot destroy the barriers in which it is caught—can exist undetected.

It is a message, and I start *to really feel* what holds the current regime together: nothing you can touch. It's an electric charge of fear crossing back and forth over lines of synapses. To be sure, it manifests concretely: infrastructure is built or destroyed, carpet bombs are scattered, every possible substance is sucked out of the ground into which whole forests sink, never to be recovered. People around you do as they're told, and you're without a home or a passport. Perhaps you end up in a safety compound.

Fear, however, is a utility without price, and a commodity no one desires—not intrinsically. It's a Sisyphean carrot at the end of a stick—a carrot that evaporates when one doesn't play by the rules. And it's driven by nothing more than numbers—not numbers, but graphic numerals—flickering on a screen.

I'm thinking of a way to escape this—to escape *this nothing*—and I am reminded of the city in which I have spent most of my life. I think of my ability to trace distinct routes each time I pass through it. I could spend a lifetime in that city, never tracing the same path twice, even through all previous destinations. And those who designed the city—and those who follow the main routes—might think that, if they wait for me at exactly the places I have been, I will return inevitably. But why should I?

It is possible the grid roads are built on nothing, and other routes—other foundations—can be built around them. Perhaps they are being built now. I see the old roads, the old grid—the ephemeral mould cast—evaporating quickly. Even more quickly than the speed at which metal rusts. The grid might dissipate, revealing what is currently undetected, what is connected now only tenuously.

I know we will soon be able to feel for these connections as if through a cloth barrier. All of us will soon find another pushing through from the other side. Hands will touch through a barrier, sensing the pulse of the other.

If we are patient, we will find a spot where the fabric has worn through.

sauna

I notice, now, that my ocean container has become very hot. Perhaps someone has turned it into a sauna. Didn't Dave say they were going to set up a sauna in the compound? Perhaps my container has been chosen for this purpose. In any event, I notice I am not alone here: beside me, on the cedar plank floor, is a slim woman who looks to be in her 40s. She wears a one-piece swimsuit, which is somehow immodest. She is stretching and doing breathing exercises. At one point she arches backward in a pose known as *Ustrasana*. Her hair is in the *Katsuyama-mage* style, bound into a ring with a white cord to reveal the nape of her neck: my favourite part of a woman's body. She seems not to be aware—or to care—that I am observing her.

Finally, after many sighs and poses, she stands up to leave. She opens the door, and I notice it is misty and snowing—it sometimes snows in April. Droplets of water fall from the top of the doorframe, and she walks through them, into the mist, onto the slush. I watch her walk away until she is no longer visible. It's a thin, muddy layer of wet snow, and I think her feet must be very damp and soiled by now. I wonder how it feels to walk on such a surface.

Perhaps I should have spoken to her, but I was too shy. Maybe I had prurient interests, and didn't want to be exposed. But why not? I'm thinking now of Yoshiko, who sometimes attracted me by wearing a thin layer of diaphanous material, because she knew I wanted something between us. That's far too personal, I know.

In any event, where am I? Has this ocean container landed in the Arctic? Perhaps I am already in transit—perhaps (even better!) on one of the Kuril Islands, waiting to be transferred.

Ryōan-ji

In Kyoto, there is a Zen temple called Ryōan-ji, in which there is a rock garden with fifteen prominent stones. From most angles on the periphery of the garden, one can see most of the stones. Only one angle, however, allows all fifteen to be seen at once. Or perhaps it is not *the angle*, but *enlightenment* that allows all fifteen stones to be seen at once. I forget which because I haven't visited Ryōan-ji in many years. The memory of my last visit is unclear—and perhaps the finer details weren't important to me at the time.

in transit

Once again, my ocean container changes, and I am certain now my comrades have saved me. Soon I will be reunited with my loved ones—and just in time. Perhaps I can start eating again. I need a change of clothes, too. The elbows of my sweater have worn through. My jeans are very loose now, and give off an unpleasant odour.

When I meet my loved ones after all these months—and once I have made myself more presentable—Yoshiko will of course be glad to see me. Perhaps Stevie will at first be confused—but within moments he'll remember who I am. A smile will emerge on his face, and then he'll run to me, yelling, "Da...da...da...!" Perhaps his language will be far more developed than that. Will he call me "papa" or "daddy"? Yoshiko will put her arms around both of us and say: "Now we are three. Let us never be apart again." Soon after we'll get jobs and build a house in the country, on stilts to avoid floodwater. It will be designed for passive cooling and have a green roof—by which I mean a garden on the roof.

I know I am in transit now because I hear a resonant, mechanical sound. An engine. Surely it is the engine of a very large boat, and I am on it. I imagine a container vessel in the middle of the north Pacific, surrounded by a vast surface of water that stretches uninterrupted to the horizon in every direction. I don't know the weather, but the ship is an almost flourescent blue—it could stand out against any maritime background. The same blue as an alpine glacier lake on a sunny morning at the height of summer. It might be called *chalfonte blue*, like the colour of a 1956 Buick Special—in case you have never seen, and from this point in history *can never see*, a lake of such colour. The boat is immense. Perhaps it is the *Emma Maersk*, to this day the largest container ship ever built. It can carry 11,000 standard units, of which my container is just *one*.

I wonder about Emma Maersk. She must be quite *hefty*, if they named the world's largest container ship after her. I feel cruel making this remark, because she may in fact be *a very nice person*. I admit to having a prejudice against the super-rich. And I feel sad for Emma Maersk, in part because I have intimate knowledge of her. I believe we went on one date together, when both of us were in our first year of university. We met by chance on campus. I was asking directions—or perhaps she was asking directions—and we struck up a conversation.

For such a wealthy person she was modest, even shy. She thought it unimportant to tell me she was a Maersk. She was wearing a long dress on the day we met, and her cleavage was very enticing. But on the appointed evening, in the back of my car (a Nissan Sentra), I did not feel the attraction I anticipated. She was enthusiastic, but our enthusiasms were poorly matched, and it made me feel sad.

Anyway, as further proof I'm in transit, I notice the door of my container can no longer be opened—I can't leave. Perhaps the security seal is on, and I'm going somewhere to be unloaded. If all this is true (it is certainly true), I think it's very clever how they've stowed me away here. It must have taken careful planning to get me inside the Emma Maersk, where I'm nothing but a grain of sand, virtually unnoticeable among all the thousands of containers.

If someone were to spy my container on the deck (presuming it were on the deck, with the identification code hidden), it would be very hard to reach. It would be like choosing a tree on a distant, forested mountain, then trying to walk to it. From inside a forest, without a vantage point (or an identification code, which trees do not have), such a task would be almost impossible.

Even more impressive is that they found a place for me *in this specific container*, sparsely packed (so I have room to move) with just one item of merchandise. I am travelling with a kind of recreational watercraft commonly known as *a jet ski*—a special order, custom made for a client in Yokohama. I know this because there is also a package of documents including an owner's manual and a letter to a "Mr. O—" that starts: "Congratulations on purchasing your new 5000cc Sea-Doo GTX Unlimited Thruster."

Upstairs, in the superstructure of the ship, I imagine a crew indifferent to this and other items of merchandise. They might be in the lounge watching videos about the sea, or monitoring the engine as it burns 14,000 litres of heavy fuel oil per hour. I can hear the engine clearly, so perhaps I am very deep in the hull. Is it possible I'm below the waterline?

I consider the vastness of the ocean. The *Emma Maersk* is alone here, exactly in the middle of the Pacific, with no other human-made points of reference. To be sure, one could argue the ocean itself is human-made— or at least modified by human activity. It has acidified. Numerous species are now extinct or near extinction because they can no longer grow exoskeletons. A billionaire has pumped iron into it. There are dead zones, where almost nothing lives. How deep is the ocean? How deep is it where I am now? There are perhaps three, four, maybe five kilometres beneath this ship. Am I over a dead zone? If not, there must be something living. And because I can't see outside this container, I listen.

a song

To distinguish individual sounds in a background of noise, one must concentrate. Musicians have found that when playing the same note or chord over and over again at a steady rate, audiences are apt to leave within ten minutes. Those who stay, however, often report hearing new sounds within the repetition—which is how I'm listening to this boat. Its engine has a main sound. It's the most obvious sound the engine makes. One notices it immediately, but it changes after listening for hours and hours on end, as I have. Now I can hear overtones, multiple overtones, and anomalies, too. Some of these anomalous sounds are from the engine itself: if it ran perfectly, predictably and always, the ship wouldn't need a crew.

But there are other sounds, and because I have listened to the engine for so long, I now can distinguish its sounds from other sounds around it. I can hear individual waves slapping against the hull, a tuna swishing its muscular tail, or a cormorant diving through the ocean's surface. What's more, I can hear these sounds not just as they happen, but even as they reverberate through the ocean for years after. That's how sensitive I have become.

I hear, too, something I can't identify—a tonal, moaning sound that starts and stops and has its own narrative arc. It seems familiar even though I am hearing it for the first time, and I wonder why I haven't noticed it until now. Has it been playing in the background all my life, so constantly that it's no more apparent than the flavour of water? I've always thought such a thing could be possible—that there might be a song that's always been playing and is so ubiquitous that one no longer hears it.

I'm quite certain now I have uncovered this invisible song. It might be an esoteric song, or it might be the same for everyone—I'm not sure. In any case, it seems like a whale song but much faster—like the recording of a large whale sped up so that it sounds like a small whale. And perhaps that is exactly what it is: the song of a small whale.

A tiny whale, even. A tiny little blue whale, just two metres long.

Acknowledgments

A previous version of "the prenatal class" appeared in *The Alarmist*. "something else," "in transit," and "a song" first appeared in *Peculiar Mormyrid*. Quoted material from Momus and The Chameleons is used by permission from Nick Currie (a.k.a. Momus) and Mark Burgess, respectively. The excerpt on page 65 is quoted from Edmund J. Bourne's *The Anxiety & Phobia Workbook* (New Harbinger, 2005), and the list on page 82 has been adapted from Kenneth Henshall's *A History of Japan: From Stone Age to Superpower* (Palgrave Macmillan, 2004).

Thank you to Ninebark Press for publishing *The Ocean Container*. Bill Mullan, Candie Tanaka, Carleigh Baker, Carolyn Chan, Clancy Dennehy, Eric Torin, Ingrid Rose, Madeleine Thien, Michael Mejia, Patricia Morris, and Steven Cline provided encouragement, editorial feedback, and other concrete assistance related to the manuscript. David Willoughby and Thea Bowering have been sounding boards since long before *The Ocean Container*. Thank you especially to Aya and Iain for giving me the space to write.

Ninebark Supporters

Ninebark Press would like to thank the following people, and our many anonymous donors, for their generous support of this book:

Anonymous (multiple)
Jason Abdelhadi
Tina Bucher & Sherre Harrington
Jeanne Cahill
Greg P. DePaco
Sarah Egerer, Brad Adams & Orgil
    Adams
Alice Friman
Rick Glenn
Susan Harvey
Jonathan Hershey
Donald A. Larson
Rachel Levy

Michael Martone
Patricia L. Morris
Mullan
Amy Pence
David James Poissant
Richard & Timea Purcell
Ray
Lance Simpson & Becky McDaniel
Scott Smith
Syd & Jodi
Cetoria Tomberlin
Eric Torin

Thank you for supporting independent publishing and new voices in contemporary writing!